From
COAL
to
SAND

Searching for Self

Rose Clayworth
Ed.D. Exeter, U.K.

BALBOA.PRESS
A DIVISION OF HAY HOUSE

Balboa Press books may be ordered through booksellers or by contacting:

Balboa Press
A Division of Hay House
1663 Liberty Drive
Bloomington, IN 47403
www.balboapress.com.au
AU TFN: 1 800 844 925 (Toll Free inside Australia)
AU Local: (02) 8310 7086 (+61 2 8310 7086 from outside Australia)

Because of the dynamic nature of the Internet, any web addresses or links contained in this book may have changed since publication and may no longer be valid. The views expressed in this work are solely those of the author and do not necessarily reflect the views of the publisher, and the publisher hereby disclaims any responsibility for them.

The author of this book does not dispense medical advice or prescribe the use of any technique as a form of treatment for physical, emotional, or medical problems without the advice of a physician, either directly or indirectly. The intent of the author is only to offer information of a general nature to help you in your quest for emotional and spiritual well-being. In the event you use any of the information in this book for yourself, which is your constitutional right, the author and the publisher assume no responsibility for your actions.

Any people depicted in stock imagery provided by Getty Images are models, and such images are being used for illustrative purposes only. Certain stock imagery © Getty Images.

Print information available on the last page.

ISBN: 978-1-9822-9038-2 (sc)
ISBN: 978-1-9822-9039-9 (e)

Balboa Press rev. date: 10/10/2023

Contents

Acknowledgements

For everyone who has helped me on my way to me.

Front and back cover photo credits: C.D.H.

Disclaimer

This story is inspired by my experience of life.

All identities and some place names have been changed.

Terminology

In England in the 1960s children in the academic school stream took subject-focussed General Certificate of Education (GCE) examinations at Ordinary ('O') Level at age 15 and Advanced ('A') Level at age 18. (Ages are approximate.)

Wisdom

The unexamined life is not worth living.
Socrates, in Plato 45

"We shall not cease from exploration
And the end of all our exploring
Will be to arrive where we started
And know the place for the first time."
T.S.Eliot, *Little Gidding*, from *Four Quartets*.

Prologue: 8 May, New Zealand

Dusk fell earlier each evening as another winter began in the Southern Hemisphere. As Rose sat in the Lazy Boy with her dog cuddling next to her, she wondered why a stultifying sense of gloom descended on her each year as May approached. Was it physical? Perhaps she suffered from Seasonal Affective Disorder, aptly abbreviated to SAD? Here in this sunny corner of New Zealand there really was very little cause for winter depression. Many Kiwis owned only rain jackets as the weather was so mild in the North Island's winter, quite different from winter in her former homeland, the UK.

Her dark mood was probably emotional. Mum had passed away in May more than a dozen years earlier, so the grief was no longer raw but the memories had not faded. The annual commemoration of ANZAC Day on the 25th of April was another depressing event. The Gallipoli Campaign had been a tragedy only outweighed by the catastrophe of "the war to end all wars". And then there was duck-shooting season, starting May 1st. The sound of gunfire reverberated across the countryside in the early morning as Rose took Bobby for his walk. It was sad to think of the wildlife dying. She could only hope the hunters killed the poor birds instantly.

Another possible trigger for this annual depression was

that May 1st was Mum's younger son's birthday. John had left the family years before Mum died. A young husband and father in his early twenties, he had struggled to cope with the breakdown of his first marriage. Rose still felt an empty hole in her heart. She vividly recalled their final words when discussing the relationship between his own children and his new partner's daughters.

"Don't give me any advice. You haven't had any kids, so you don't know what it's like."

Deeply hurt, Rose had retaliated sharply. "I know you don't like taking advice. You've fallen out with Mum for the same reason. So I'll let you work it out for yourself."

Rose now wished she had been more patient with her 'baby brother', 15 years younger than herself. He had had a difficult relationship with Mum since his teens, but it was hard to work out why he had felt the complete rupture of their relationship to be necessary. Perhaps he couldn't handle the family situation any longer. A single parent with incipient rheumatoid arthritis (RA) when her youngest child was born, becoming steadily more severely disabled, Mum wasn't easy to live with. She was ultimately unable to leave the house alone and needed help with basic daily tasks. She lived life at one stage removed from reality, struggling to control the pain in her twisted joints. Like a butterfly trapped in the chrysalis stage physically, she was mentally all too aware of her predicament, having had her glory days when she was young and lovely. She didn't give way to anger often, but when she did, her children knew it.

Rose, too, experienced sudden violent rages. Whether the behaviour was learned from observation, or genetic, a personality trait, she wanted to modify her 'over the top' reaction to challenges. Examining her life journey might help, though it would be impossible to rationalise cause and effect. "I'll start at the beginning," she told herself, "and try to unravel the strands of my tapestry. I'll effect my own writing cure for my depression and tantrums."

1

Early Childhood

ROSE AND BILL'S childhood had been shattered by the breakup of their parents' marriage. Only 11 and 9 years old, the two children had watched and listened as Mum and Dad argued their way towards legal separation, then experienced the physical split from their familiar surroundings and the silence as uncontested divorce proceedings took place. Yet their very early childhood had been happy, Rose recalled. The crumpled black and white family photos showed two contented small children, three-year-old Bill pedalling his new American Jeep, and five-year-old Rose feeding custard cream biscuit 'sandwiches' and Mars bar 'cake' slices to her little brother, her dolly and Teddies as they sat around her on a blanket on the front lawn of their small, single-storey home in Hopewell.

Hopewell village was constructed post-World War 2 with prefabricated single-storey bungalows to speedily accommodate mineworkers, some of whom had been continuously employed at Hopewell Colliery during the War. Jack, Rose's Dad, had been one of those. A fourteen-year-old boy when he started work in the Colliery, he and his four siblings lived with their parents in a two-storey brick-built house in the older, purpose-built National Colliery village just outside the 'pit' gates. As an adult he sometimes complained about having to stay at work during the War, instead of being allowed to join the armed forces. The oldest of four brothers and one sister he had been born in Cumberland soon after the end of World War 1, on a farm he still held dear in his mind's eye. But as a young boy his father and mother had made their way on foot to the expanding Hopewell Colliery in Derbyshire.

The family had been fortunate to be housed in the romantically named village of Berry Vale. After completing a rudimentary education at his country school, Jack had been sent to the mine to earn his living like his father. He had eventually achieved the status of 'fitter', or mechanic, and spent a working lifetime in the mines, but he never forgave his parents for sending him to work in the colliery in the early '30s. When WW2 broke out in 1939, Jack was compelled to continue in the mines as coal provided energy for the industries which women operated while their men were fighting in Europe. Jack would rather have followed his younger brother into the Air Force as a gunner. Although aware that his brother might never have come home, the disappointment remained deep in his heart.

Jack found love in his late twenties with a young woman who also had disappointments in her life. They had married just after the end of the War. Mary, the youngest of twelve children, was 19, desperate to get away from home. Her father Dick, a farm labourer, had met his future bride, May, when he lodged in her parents' house in Nottinghamshire. Their married life with a dozen children could not have been easy, but May could not have guessed that her young husband would become a drunkard who abused her. The family lived in a small, two-storey stone cottage next to the farm where Dick worked. In her old age the farmer's wife disapprovingly recalled the bad behaviour May had put up with until her youngest child, Mary, got married and had her own home. Surprisingly, Dick's heavy drinking did not bring on an early death after his wife left him. Rose had only one memory of her maternal grandfather and it was positive. He had taken part with his horse and cart in the Hopewell carnival parade, when Mum had dressed her as the Queen of Hearts, with a white frock and a red heart-trimmed apron and bonnet. She was only about four at the time and although there was no photograph of the event, the memory of the pretty fancy dress costume and of riding in the cart was still vivid.

As a child Rose was not aware of the negativity of the relationship between her Mum and her Grandpa. Of course she now knew the reasons for his absence from her life but Grandpa Dick died when she was only six. On the other hand, maternal Grandma May had played an important part in her childhood. May had lived with her children on a rotating basis after leaving her husband. Although money matters were never mentioned in front of children, in 1948 the Basic State Pension replaced the old Poor Law with its threat of the Workhouse but it was minimal and probably not available to a non-working wife separated from her husband. May had travelled around the UK staying with each of her married children, helping them by cooking, cleaning and providing babysitting services. She was white-haired, short in stature and the years of childbearing had thickened her

3

figure but what she had lost in looks she made up for in culinary skills. Rose recalled that she made wonderful meat and potato pies, although meat, still a rationed ingredient in the post-War years, did not figure largely. They were really potato and meat pies. May had spent some time at Mary and Jack's house in Hopewell both before and after the birth of Bill. Rose remembered the scare when Mum had developed scarlet fever while heavily pregnant with Bill. She had gone into an isolation ward in hospital till the baby was born. The birth went well, though Bill had been a sickly baby. He did not 'thrive' as the parlance went, but he made it through those difficult first years. Rose treasured photos of herself as a toddler with Mum and Grandma with baby Bill in her arms. They represented the happy early days of her life.

Relationships with some of Mum's older siblings who lived nearby were quite strong, though Dad's siblings didn't play much of a part in the children's lives. Uncle Ned and Aunty Pru had two daughters, Polly and Andrea. Another photo showed the terror Rose experienced riding a seaside donkey with her legs trapped by the cousins' donkeys on either side of her. The memory of rough hair pressing hard against her legs still made her shudder. Other very early memories were of the old house Uncle Ned lived in where Grandma stayed when Rose was tiny. It was a two-storey house with an unusual configuration in which the cousins' bedroom led off from Grandma's bedroom. Rose recalled staying the night, sleeping in the big feather bed with Grandma, and smelling her nightly glass of Wincarnis 'tonic' wine before trying to sleep without slipping down the steep slope which Grandma's body made in the soft feather mattress. In the morning Rose had hot porridge oats for breakfast in a bunny rabbit-decorated dish. Aunty Pru encouraged her to eat quickly by pointing out that the promenading bunny rabbit family couldn't breathe while they were covered in porridge. Rose might have been affected by the anxiety this created in her developing mind. She still hated any form of animal neglect, even the mildest, and was also a vegetarian.

Rose had another visual clip in her memory from that period. It was of herself, on her garden swing at the age of four or five, with a clear view into the kitchen of the Hopewell prefab in the afternoon. The dayshift at the mine ended around 3pm, and when Dad came home, Rose saw Mum embrace him, putting her arms around his neck, while he bent down to kiss her. There was not a lot of physicality in the family, so the image of their earlier, happy relationship had burned itself into her mind. It became an arbiter of her own future emotional experience, a criterion against which she measured the depth of her feelings. All her adult life she longed to experience the closeness and joy of being at one with a partner which she had glimpsed in that brief moment. The other person in the visual memory had been her childhood friend, Aled Jones, or Hanging Bones as she had called him. Her linguistic capacity for rhyme and rhythm was strong even as a young child. Aled was the son of the neighbours, Muriel and Peter. One day Aled had pushed her too high on the garden swing and she had been thrown out of the seat, but her fingers had stayed trapped in the chains which suspended it. She could still recall the pain in her torn fingernails and the burn of the chain on her palms. She didn't recall swinging with him again after that. 'Once bitten, twice shy,' was still her motto. Be careful. Stay away from danger.

Mum had not been able to attend secondary school, one of her big disappointments in life, because Grandma couldn't afford to buy the requisite uniform. Another regret was her thwarted desire to go with her friend, Trisha, to the Victory in Europe Day celebrations in London. Grandma had not given the teenager permission. Mary recalled that Trisha had met a handsome Canadian soldier in Trafalgar Square, married him and emigrated to a new life. Mary never got over losing her chance to escape her small known world. Rose guessed that Mum had wanted her daughter to have a better life than she had had.

Rose had another enduring memory of learning to read at the early age of three. Mum had not been much of a reader herself, she had preferred practical pastimes, such as knitting, sewing and crochet, at all of which she became an expert. Yet, as a new young mother Mary invested a lot of time in teaching her firstborn to read. Rose remembered sitting on her mother's knee, with an *Old Lob* book, reading aloud the simple stories about country life. Some of the black and white pictures in the little book still hovered around the edge of her mind, but a negative memory of learning to read centred on one word. She could still see *begun* in large lower case font on the small page. In her three-year-old mind those five letters made two words she already knew: *be* and *gun*. But her infant logic could not work out the meaning of *be gun*. No doubt in her elementary mental lexicon she was familiar with the word *started*, rather than *begun*. Mum had become extremely angry at what she believed was an easy word. The little girl on her knee almost cried with frustration. She didn't want to be chastised for making mistakes. Would she be wrong if she said *be gun*? After an awful pause filled with Mum's angry words, she spoke the syllables she saw, and Mum was pleased. But Rose was totally perplexed. She had no idea what those two little words meant.

That painful memory had faded with time and only been resurrected when Rose began studying educational psychology as part of her postgraduate teaching diploma. But there was another one, which had surfaced later, when she studied the intricacies of English grammar which native speakers are blissfully ignorant of. It was a religious memory, too, which agnostic Rose now found laughable. Mum had insisted on her little girl saying her prayers, kneeling at the end of the bed. She had learned to say the child's prayer:

Gentle Jesus, meek and mild, Look upon a little child.
Pity my simplicity. Suffer me to come to thee.

The entire prayer was a challenge to a beginning reader, but the syntax and the archaic lexis of line three could not be cognitively processed by the verbally limited young mind. So Rose had converted that line in the prayer to something she could understand: *Pity me to simple city.* For the remainder of her young life when she was made to recite the prayer she wondered where the simple city could be. Like so many other issues children ask about, such as "Where do babies come from?" only to be told "You'll find out when you are grown up." Rose just put the question in her mental filing cabinet and hoped to learn the answer one day. Now she laughed about it.

As a young mother Mum was a rigid disciplinarian, typical of the times. She had a job in the Berry Vale primary school before she was married, as assistant to the kindergarten teacher. So as a three-year-old Rose had been able to start kindergarten earlier than normal. At first Mum must have taken her to school on the bus from Hopewell, but as she got older Rose travelled on her own. One terrible day when the weather had warmed up she had forgotten to take her coat from its peg in the school cloakroom for the afternoon bus ride home. She must have done this more than once, because on that awful day, Mum had not allowed her to come into the house, shouting at her that she had to go back to school to get it. It was heartbreaking for Rose to visualise her five-year-old self crying on the doorstep. The outcome was no longer clear, but she probably learned from the trauma to pick up her coat from the cloakroom even on hot days. Obeying rules was still important to adult Rose.

Those early childhood years must have played a part in establishing Rose's personality, but the memories were retrieved as if looking at snapshots in a photo album. Other telling information was provided by Mum's reminiscences, especially about Rose's love for food. Apparently, once Rose's baby feeding bottle of warm milk was empty, she would throw it out of her pram, often breaking it. As a result, Mum substituted empty HP (Houses of Parliament) Sauce bottles for the more expensive glass baby bottles. Mature Rose recognized that sense of frustration when a comforting drink was finished, only now the bottle was whisky or wine!

One early photo of the two children could explain Rose's ongoing fear of heights. Wearing a pretty hand-smocked dress, Rose aged about four and her two-year-old brother were seated precariously on the slippery, polished wood, dining table. The wary look in the little girl's eyes hinted at her fear, and her hands were firmly holding on to the younger child. Obviously Rose's love for her brother, her reading ability, interest in languages and her fear of heights as well as her greed and impetuous nature were all apparent in early childhood but the years from six onwards also had their impact on the formation of Rose's character. The old nursery rhyme was apt:

There was a little girl who had a little curl, right in the middle of her forehead.

When she was good, she was very very good but when she was bad she was horrid.

2

Primary School

WHEN ROSE WAS six, Dad rented a larger, brick-built, two-storey house in the mining village at the 'pit-gates' where his parents lived. The purpose-built colliery village was not as pastoral as the name suggested, but living there made Rose's journey to school very short indeed. The walk took around five minutes. This meant that forgetting a coat, or not taking swim things, could easily be remedied. In the new, larger house Mum had become even more 'house proud' than in the small prefab, investing long hours cleaning and polishing the floors, windows and heavy wooden furniture. As a young girl with a duster in hand Rose bitterly resented the black coal dust which crept inside the windows and lay on the cream gloss paint of the windowsills. She and Bill had made a game of polishing the light brown linoleum by tying yellow dusters to their feet and sliding around as if ice-skating, something they could never afford to do in reality.

In fact, that very early start at school, three years in advance of children of her own age, had not done Rose much good. She had left the kindergarten early as she could already read at age three. She had then moved up through the levels each year, including the horrible experience with the female teacher in the third class, who made her wash her mouth out with soap for using a swear word she could no longer recall. Her parents never swore, so it was a mystery how Rose learned a word bad enough to merit punishment. Eventually Rose had spent three years in the final primary school class with a kindly, elderly spinster teacher. She had virtually become this teacher's class assistant, working as a monitor giving out teaching materials and taking the 'eleven plus' secondary school selection examination practice tests three times. It was no surprise that she had passed the real test and was enrolled in the 'grammar' school in the nearest county town when she was twelve.

Recently, while trying to organise her heavily laden bookshelves, Rose had come across the leather-bound text which had been awarded her for succeeding in the 'eleven plus' exam: Jane Austen's *Northanger Abbey*. On reading the handwritten inscription, tears had come to her eyes when she realised how precious that teacher's quiet support had been. Even as she endured the same curriculum three times over Rose had enjoyed the Friday afternoon stories from *Worzel Gummidge*, read aloud to the whole class. Her own voracious reading habit had never abated and her interest in learning was undimmed.

Physically and emotionally Rose had experienced some negatives in primary school. A young girl's first period starting while at school is a challenge, but living so close to school Rose could go home and find the necessary sanitary belt and napkin to wear for the monthly 'curse'. Mum had warned her about it and had planned for it, knowing her daughter was the tallest in her class. Adult Rose was grateful for early menopause.

Swimming lessons with school were another uncomfortable memory for Rose. Her eyesight had been identified as minus 7.5 in each eye at the age of six. From then on she had to wear ugly plastic-framed National Health glasses which meant name calling at school. The cry of 'spekky four eyes' gave Rose an inferiority complex which she had never shaken off. Poor eyesight made going to the swimming baths as a schoolchild a nightmare. Having taken off her glasses to swim, she could hardly see, and the echoing cries of children swimming, and the splashing sounds of them jumping into the water, made the whole environment exaggeratedly noisy and scary. As a consequence she had barely learned to swim, only just achieving the required width with approximately eleven strokes. Swimming in the sea was not an option in landlocked Derbyshire so she had not suffered from the deficiency. On rare seaside holidays on the East Coast the sea was cold and grey, so by no means tempting.

Tall Rose was good at games such as netball and she could handle a ball well in 'rounders', but she was afraid of heights. She hated gym, where she was supposed to jump the 'horse' and climb ropes and wall bars. She enjoyed taking nature walks in the local woods which bordered the school premises. There was also fun to be had in the playground with skipping ropes, singing songs such as *The big ship sails on the Ally Ally O*, about Christopher Columbus crossing the Atlantic Ocean *on the last day of September*, hopscotch and circle games, such as *The Farmer Wants a Wife*, *In and out the dusky bluebells*, and *Ring a Ring o' Roses* - a tragic echo from the 1665 epidemic of the Plague in the Derbyshire village of Eyam - but the children were blissfully ignorant of that sad history.

From about nine years old Rose's best friend was Angela, who lived over the crest of the hill on which the village was constructed. The other side of the hill, a walk of about 750 metres, was a huge geographical stride for a child. Angela was dark-haired, dark-eyed, attractive, vivacious and bright. The two girls liked to dress in the same clothes, keeping up with the fashion of the late '50s, Capri pants, and flared skirts with cinched waists and starched petticoats made of 'paper nylon' to make them swing out. Mum didn't share Rose's interest in fashion. Although her own clothes were pretty, she probably felt it was not necessary to spend much on the wardrobe of a child. One horrific item she bought without consulting Rose was a multicoloured, vividly striped dress, more suitable for a clown in Rose's eyes.

Mum became seriously interested in ballroom dancing at this point in time, and went to classes at the Hopewell Hotel a short walk from home. Rose wondered now who had been her dancing partner. It was certainly not Dad. Mum had achieved a Bronze Medal but never spoke about it. After the weekly lessons there was a social dance, which Rose had sometimes attended. She enjoyed doing the Gay Gordons, the Veleta and the Military Two Step, but she hated the shoes she had to wear. Mum had kept Rose in brown leather lace-up shoes until she was ten. Rose's first pair of longed for 'winkle pickers', flats with exaggeratedly pointed toes, were bought when she was 11. They were amazing to look at, but not so comfortable to wear. Just as Mum had warned, Rose's fourth toe on each foot was partly folded under the third as a result of wearing them while her feet were still growing. Young Rose liked to muse that she could become a ballerina as she had the physical advantage of her first three toes being equal in length. But family finances had not allowed her to take ballet classes, and by the age of 12 Rose had reached 5' 8", two inches taller than the preferred height for a ballerina. Also, there was her need to wear glasses to see further than a hand in front of her face: not a good stage look.

As the two girlfriends grew older boyfriends began to appear on the village scene. Church choir attendance at Mattins and Evensong on Sundays brought a couple of interesting Hopewell boys into their lives. Ted was good-looking with dark, curly hair, of average height and stocky in build. He had a cute little terrier which went everywhere with him. Toby had lighter coloured, straight hair which flipped onto his forehead. He was tall and slim with fine facial features. Both boys were well-behaved, and were welcomed at home but who knew what might have happened if Rose had had more free time?

From the age of 12 she was busy with grammar school homework, so the two girls mainly got together at the weekend, to roller skate on the streets or sing pop songs at home. Singing was something Rose revelled in still. She had performed at age six as the Virgin Mary with her baby Jesus doll, singing the Christmas Carol *We will rock you*, while balancing precariously on a stage made up of wooden classroom desks. At twelve she was a member of the church choir and also a trainee church bell ringer. Choir practice was on Wednesday evenings in a nearby village, and bell-ringing was on Thursday evenings up at the medieval church. On Sundays Rose loved singing hymns in the ancient, atmospheric building. Mum was a believer, though Dad was an atheist. One Evensong Rose experienced a vision of being a missionary, though the idea was soon forgotten. Walking to church through the woods was a great time to catch up with her best friend. The strong smell of wild garlic plants featured in those memories. The woods were redolent of the scent in spring and summer. Their white flowers were replaced with a carpet of bluebells in spring, a lovely sight and a much more pleasant fragrance!

The school holidays in summer seemed in retrospect to have always been fine and endlessly long. Rose smilingly recalled one summer holiday when they both had matching bikes: Angela's painted purple, and Rose's pink. They filled up the front handlebar drinks-carriers with lemonade and packed sandwiches to go for a long ride and a picnic into the countryside. Most summer vacations were spent at home but twice they went on holiday together, Angela joining Rose, her Mum and Bill at a caravan park on the East Coast for a week, and Rose going on a two-week motor camping trip around the North and South Devon coasts with Angela. Both holidays were enjoyable but the amazing motor tour gave Rose an idea of how different family life could be and how wonderful the South West of England was, compared to the landlocked county and coalfields of Derbyshire. She loved the freedom of travelling by car because her parents did not own one. She did not even know if her Dad could drive. Angela's parents were a likeable couple, but her older brother was a dark enigma. He didn't talk much, rather like Rose's uncle, Dad's youngest brother, Dean, who was not much older than Rose. Both teenage boys probably thought these two younger girls were in a different world from their own, though Gran had a TV and encouraged Rose to come and watch the 6.05 Special program, an innovative pop music program which Dean enjoyed too.

Another friend Rose recalled from the halcyon days in Berry Vale was next-door neighbour Jackie. The two girls enjoyed the pop songs of the time, and had great fun sitting on Dad's empty hen house in the back garden, swinging their legs as they sang *Green Door*, imagining themselves famous like the Beverly and Kay sisters. Then there was the local shopkeeper's daughter. She was the same age as Rose, and her younger brother was around Bill's age. So it was not surprising that their parents became friends, even going on a day trip together once. Rose treasured a photo of Mum at the time looking exotic in dark glasses and a strappy sundress. Other photos showed the four adults in swimming costumes, obviously relaxed and happy, while the girls wore sandals and sundresses on that memorable seaside visit. Rose loved the sea, even though she found the vast expanse of moving water frightening. The clean sea breeze was infinitely preferable to the coal dust-ridden atmosphere back at home.

There was a darker memory attached to the shop, however. The family went away on holiday once and left Mum in charge of the shop for a week. Greedy Rose was tempted by the easy access to confectionery, so every time Mum took her to the shop, she sneaked a couple of sweets for herself. Becoming emboldened in her undetected petty crime spree, she daringly took a small triangular paper bag that held two ounces of sweets and filled it with 'red lips', sherbet lemons, and 'space ships', a novelty sherbet sweet. She hid the bag in Dad's garden shed, in a drawer he hardly ever opened as it stuck. The shed loomed guiltily in Rose's memory even after she had managed to secretly consume the goodies. The guilt lingered and recurred at odd moments. She never confessed this to anyone and soon afterwards the shop was sold and the family moved away. Adult Rose, filled with shame, wondered whether they had noticed that some sweets were missing. It was hardly likely, but there was no more contact. Rose sometimes wondered what happened to their friends, but she had never looked them up. The repressed guilt probably affected her memory of them negatively.

Rose's paternal grandmother lived right outside the school gates, even closer than the family house. Visiting Gran became a regular treat. She always made Camp Coffee with milk on Sunday mornings, and gave the young children a saucerful of the delicious, sweet, creamy drink. Drinking from a saucer in retrospect seemed rather strange. Perhaps it was an economy, restricting the quantity of the drink, as well as ensuring the children didn't drink coffee that was too hot. Probably Gran didn't have kid-size cups. There was also a memory of a dog, like an Airedale Terrier in its huge proportions, but Dad said it was a smaller version, a Lakeland. Rose remembered its imposing stance at the top of the steep steps up to Gran's house. She could not recall any barking or biting but it still frightened her as a little girl. Perhaps she had a residual memory of the first large dog she ever came eye to eye with as a toddler at her Aunt Heather's house, where her Uncle Ron was chief stableman to the Essex Hunt and Hounds. Mum and Rose lived with Heather until Jack obtained the prefab in which they could begin their married life. Rose was still slightly afraid of big dogs.

Happy family memories of Berry Vale included long walks in a nearby country house estate, particularly to visit the annual fair with motorised carnival rides, such as a carousel and a 'waltzer', which came in late summer. When Bill got tired of walking, Dad would put him on his shoulders. At other times, Dad and Mum took them to pick hazel nuts or elderberries in the woods, with which Mum made elderberry wine. She also made raspberry vinegar and blackcurrant jam from the fruit Dad grew in his garden. Rose smiled as she thought of her own garage full of preserves and fruit wine. Gardening gave Dad a lot of pleasure after the long hours underground in the mine. Also it helped feed the family. Food in the post-War years was not plentiful. Rose remembered the ration cards, and the concentrated orange juice and cod liver oil in small bottles for families with children. Dad was a huge consumer of cod liver oil. He could drink a whole bottle in one go! He swore it helped him bring up the coal dust which settled on his chest after a shift. It may well have been true, since even after retirement he had only a small amount of pneumoconiosis, or dust on the lungs.

Once a week, Mum would go food shopping to the Cooperative Store on Hopewell Hill which gave discounts to Coop members. There Rose gazed in wonder at the huge mounds of fresh butter from which the assistants made neat pats for their customers and the equally gargantuan whole round cheeses which the shopgirls cut with a wire into neat slices of the requested size. A special treat was a can of Creamola, effervescent crystals which dissolved in water to make lemonade. The only other soft drink Rose recalled from her early childhood was the mysteriously named Dandelion and Burdock. As a child she had wondered how these two weed plants could be made into a sweet, fizzy drink. Purchases were paid for with cash placed into an aerial tube with the invoice and sent to the cashier, who sent the change and receipt whizzing back over the customers' heads. It was fascinating for a child to behold.

However, home food was not exciting. Rose had clear memories of boxed, processed, Dairy Lea cream cheese and its sister product, bright orange Velveeta. Rose preferred the more natural-looking spread which was used in sandwiches or on toast. Bill hated eating meat, which was only served on Sunday anyway, but he was very keen on canned baked beans or spaghetti on toast. Or so Mum thought. She bought three small cans of Heinz beans and three of spaghetti from the mobile grocery van which paid a weekly visit to the village. Its prices were cheaper and sometimes products were more modern than those held in the shops, such as Smiths Potato Crisps, flavoured with salt the consumer sprinkled onto the potatoes from a twist of blue greaseproof paper. They were a longed for treat. As for every day meals, not many stood out for Rose, although there was an apocryphal story about Bill's chosen menu.

"Beans or spaghetti?" Mum would ask as she prepared Bill's teatime toast. "Spaghetti, please, Mum," Bill would answer without fail. One day, in quiet desperation, he asked Mum. "When will I finish the spaghetti?" She realised in a light bulb moment that he actually preferred beans but felt he had to use up the spaghetti cans first!

During their early childhood Bill and Rose had been

as close as different gender siblings are likely to be. Rose had felt a strong maternal instinct for her brother but they also played imaginative games together, or had 'feet fights' on their beds in their shared bedroom. One early Sunday morning when Mum and Dad were still asleep the children decided to fly to the moon on the household vacuum cleaner, a much prized modern gadget, made by Goblin. This cylinder of black steel and shining silver chrome was stored high up in the small third bedroom on the raised 'box' over the staircase below. Dad kept his beloved vinyl records there but the children didn't notice them as they climbed onto the 'space rocket'. As they blasted off, the disks began to fall with a horrendous crash. The resulting 'telling off' was severe. Luckily Dad's *Banana Boat Song* by Nat King Cole was saved, but others, like Lonnie Donegan's *Cumberland Gap* were cracked.

Another time young Rose had searched for Christmas presents in a high cupboard. The box with a set of dolls' tea party crockery made of delicate white porcelain, crashed to the floor, breaking its contents. Mum's anger taught Rose an important lesson about good behaviour but to her amazement and endless gratitude on the big day she was given a not so pretty but much more substantial pottery set.

3

Grammar School

WHEN ROSE PASSED the infamous 'eleven plus' exam which separated children into academic or technical secondary school populations, she was registered at an all girls' high school. Next door was the single sex boys' school. The hedge which divided the schools at the end of their properties, far away from school buildings and supervising teachers, was populated heavily at break and lunchtimes with girls and boys posting notes through the shrubs. Rose did not participate in this. She had no boyfriend, just friends who were boys. The grammar school children from Berry Vale were driven the 15 miles into town on a small private bus where friendships developed between the student commuters. One friend was Jane, also from Berry Vale but older. With Jane playing the guitar accompaniment, she and Rose performed a duet for the school Christmas Concert in her second year. They sang *Dream*, a pop hit by the Everly Brothers, which Rose had received on a small, vinyl record greetings card, for her birthday!

Rose loved music just as Mum and Dad did: Mum preferred Jim Reeves, Dad liked skiffle and calypso. After

Rose's debut as the singing Virgin Mary, at age six she had begun learning to play the piano. Mum managed to scrape together two sterling pounds and 40 pennies for eight thirty minute lessons with Mr Farmer who lived one street down the hill. His house, though small, was impressive: His grand piano took up almost all the space in his sitting room. He was an amazing pianist and a kindly teacher. Rose very much admired the grand piano and still aspired to own one, even though both the size and cost were prohibitive.

Despite her young age Rose had progressed very well with classical music study and when she was ten or eleven Mum rather surprisingly, given the expense involved, decided she should try modern music. Perhaps Mum was influenced by the success which Winifred Atwell was experiencing as a 'boogie woogie' pianist at the time! Russ Conway was also making his name with popular music and Liberace had performed on TV with his candelabra and grand piano. So Rose was enrolled for a jazz music lesson once a week in a nearby village. She enjoyed learning to 'vamp' and took to the idea of syncopation, but after memorising *Smoke gets in your eyes*, she found time to practise limited by high school homework. So Rose gave up her piano studies. She could read music well enough to play for pleasure and to sing contralto in harmony, so Mum was satisfied with her investment, Rose hoped.

In her first year of high school, Rose found herself enjoying most subjects. Latin was not difficult and French was easy for her, but the teacher, a Frenchwoman, upset her. Madame refused to allow Rose to use her own name in class, but gave her another: Mireille. Mireille Mathieu was enjoying contemporary success as a singer, but Rose found the name unpronounceable, and so hated roll call, when she had to say her name out loud. History was fun because the teacher was every girl's idea of a heart-throb. A Bryan Ferry type, this young, handsome teacher lived in Nottingham. He drove a small white car which Rose had seen passing through her village on the Nottingham road. The actual content of history lessons seemed rather boring. On the other hand, English literature was interesting, while Algebra and Geometry were tricky but General Science was acceptable. The school had an excellent academic reputation and despite her strengths and weaknesses Rose had no doubt that she would do well there. She was made Form Captain in her second year, so expected to go to university, although no one she knew had done so.

She also learned some important life lessons at school. From the first week she had become part of a solid foursome with three girls from the town. They were all pretty, with blue eyes, and none of them wore glasses. Rose felt like the ugly duckling among them, and could not understand why they liked her. Their surnames all coincided in the register, one after the alphabetical other, so perhaps their friendship was forged literally or numerically. Although they were not aware of it until they made the round of sleepovers at each other's houses, two of them were Roman Catholic, while the other two were weakly and weekly Anglican. Carol was the first to issue an invitation to stay on Saturday night. Her house was in the wealthy, 'stockbroker belt'. She was an only child, tall, beautiful, blonde, with high cheekbones and clear blue eyes with long lashes. She was slim, but gangly still at age 13, and a star at netball. She had the potential to be a top model, but seemed humbly unaware of her beauty.

At Carol's house Rose felt as if she had entered the *Secret Garden* of Frances Burnett Hodgson. The house and garden were huge and full of intriguing nooks and crannies. It was a house to aspire to, Rose thought. Carol's parents seemed different too, more sophisticated and much better spoken than her own, though warm and friendly. After this visit Rose had several nights wrestling with her conscience about being ashamed of her own much humbler home and origins, before being able to ask her friends over. She took consolation from the Bible, muttering, "It is better to give than receive," to herself, to cool her face, flushed with embarrassment at the thought of the other girls' reactions. Next they visited Lois' home, which was out in the country and very different from Rose's in size and prettiness. Once again Rose had to struggle with self-consciousness about her home's material shortcomings.

After that, they visited Charlotte's home in the suburbs, a house similar to Rose's own, but with several more children living it. The atmosphere was crowded and chaotic, but happy. The final visit was to Rose's own small piece of rented mining property. Mum went full out on the cleaning before the visit, so the house was pristine when the girls arrived on Saturday. Then there was an exciting walk in the wood on their own. When they got back they found Mum had made blackcurrant jam, which she served warm on vanilla ice cream slices. The girls were in raptures over this special treat. On Sunday morning the two Catholic girls were faced with a problem: If they didn't go to church they would have to confess to a 'mortal' sin the following week. So they all took the bus to town and went to the Catholic Church. It was the first time Rose saw an incense censer.

She had much to think about in terms of sin, confession and how the Church governed the other girls' lives, rather than guided their values and attitudes as the Anglican Church did. She was later to recall this memory when her own wedding was in question, as her husband-to-be was Catholic and wished her to convert.

This friendship broke up once Rose had left the school after her parents' separation. But she still retained a fond memory of the warmth of the relationship. She mused on how different her own life might have been if she had stayed at this academic all girls school, where she had begun to learn Greek as well as Latin. Several girls went to Oxford or Cambridge. Schoolgirl Rose could only pray that her own hopes for university study would be fulfilled.

4

Paradise Lost

AS ROSE SETTLED into her happy secondary school life, fate stepped in and changed its course irrevocably. Mum and Dad began to fight verbally. Grandma came to stay for a while, perhaps to deflect the children's attention from their parents' unhappiness. Mum and Dad, she knew, had not always been in agreement. They had a little black and white fox terrier, spoiled by Mum's silliness according to Dad. He was an intelligent little dog, but he behaved badly, often running away onto the main road, stopping traffic. When he became uncontrollable Dad took him to be euthanased. The children and Mum were inconsolable. Other parental rows had been trivial in comparison. Mum told Rose much later that she had wanted an electric iron, but Dad had not allowed the purchase. He thought the flat iron heated on the coal fire was good enough. This had not gone down well with Mum. On another occasion Dad had gone on a motorbike holiday with some male friends. They had travelled to Scotland, leaving Mum at home with the two children. On his return, Dad presented Mary with a brooch in the shape of a horseshoe with lucky purple heather on it, and the inscription MOTHER written across it. Mum had flung it back at him, shouting "I'm not your mother!"

Rose had picked the brooch up and put it in her own jewellery box, a model of a wooden Swiss chalet, with a little ballerina who danced as the music played when you lifted the roof lid. Mum had lined the box with black velvet. Rose still treasured the box. The brooch, however, had disappeared. Rose loved jewellery. As a child, she enjoyed taking her treasures, especially her silver ballerina charm bracelet, out of the box and looking at them, much as Bill enjoyed counting his threepenny bits saved in an old *Zube* cough sweets tin. One Aunt gave her a selection of huge costume jewellery rings, which Rose delighted in and wore throughout her university years. These items were now lost. A little Welsh doll brooch was another missing treasure. It had been bought when the family visited Mt. Snowdon. Rose vividly recalled the little figure with a tall black hat, a black dress and shoes, and a red cape and white pinafore, beautifully enamelled in gleaming red, black and white.

She remembered that holiday in North Wales for two reasons: the trip up the mountain on the small gauge railway and more dramatically, Bill's accident. They had been staying at Rhyll Miners' Holiday Camp in rooms with glass doors and large hooks on posts to hold the doors open in the breeze. Bill had fallen on one of the hooks and sustained an injury to his forehead. Although not needing hospital treatment he wore a large bandage on his head for a while.

Rose's beloved baby doll, Rosebud by name and by manufacture, had suffered a different fate. Mum had made lots of Rose's clothes, and for each dress, Rosebud had received a copy in miniature. Rose had taken the little blue-eyed doll and her 'wardrobe' with her to Kuwait when she married, but the doll had been looted, along with most other possessions in the 1990 invasion. Rose still treasured the two items of clothing which remained: a small checked wool dressing gown and a pair of tiny striped navy and white cotton bloomers. Her white Teddy Bear with pink ears, which doubled as a nightdress case, suffered the same fate. It was not the material value of the items lost which mattered to Rose, but the emotional loss of treasured possessions with sentimental significance. Those who have lost a home to fire, or possessions to burglars, know the hole that is left in the memory and heart as a result.

Although there had been bad times as well as good in their childhood spent with Dad, in her selective memory the good outweighed the bad for the most part. Rose's close relationship with her brother had helped maintain continuity. Bill might have felt it was too close, as he had been the subject of her early motivation to teach. As soon as she had learned to read and was enjoying Grimm's illustrated fairy tales as well as tales of *Noddy in Toytown* and other Enid Blyton books, she felt the need to teach Bill. So when he was only two, he was subjected to reading lessons. Similarly, when Rose started the piano at age six, Bill, aged four, had to experience piano lessons.

Both children became avid readers, visiting the lending library on their own in a nearby town every week to change their books, but Bill, despite his stoic acceptance, never became a pianist. Later in life they both shared precious memories of their lost children's books, especially their *Rupert the Bear* and *Beano* albums, received as birthday or Christmas gifts, probably given away by generous Mum to some more needy family. Mum had always saved money carefully during the year so as to give her two children special gifts on birthdays and Christmas but once the children had 'outgrown them' they were given away to charity.

One toy stuck in Rose's memory still, an early Disney film spin off: a wind up dancing Cinderella and Prince Charming. Rose loved to start the couple up and watch them waltz but one day she inspected the toy more closely. To her surprise she found that Prince Charming was balanced on Cinderella's base and could be lifted off: Cinderella could dance alone. This unwitting symbol of female independence lay in Rose's subconscious and was reinforced by her Mum's actions.

Mary was gifted with a childlike sense of fun which was demonstrated in positive and generous ways despite her limited housekeeping budget. As well as buying exciting Christmas presents, at Easter she always arranged a splendid selection of eggs, some with spun sugar scenes and coloured flowers, others with chocolates inside, or sugar pigs, ceramic animal eggcups or mugs, for the children to find on the dining table on Easter Sunday morning. But she also had a darker side, perhaps stemming from her own deprived childhood. For example, she sometimes stirred her hot tea with a spoon and then touched it briefly to one of the children's bare arms. No physical damage was done, but seeing the shock on the child's face made Mum laugh out loud. Of course, it didn't seem funny to the lightly scalded child, who learned not to trust her. Mary also had a tendency to punish her children by refusing to speak to them if they had been naughty. This 'sulking' kind of punishment was worse for Rose emotionally than the physical beatings with the balloon stick they endured when they were disobedient, such as reading with their flashlights under the bedsheets instead of going to sleep at night. We all know how hard it is to wake up tired children for school in the mornings, so adult Rose empathised with her young Mum to some extent.

In her private moments Rose dreamed her own dreams. In her reading she had come across the mystic Orient through the tales of Sinbad the Sailor and Ali Baba and the Forty Thieves. In school she wrote a story with her own illustrations which referenced the excitement these stories stirred in her, though there was a memorable error when she wrote about thieves using gelatine instead of gelignite to gain entry to a treasure house! In the privacy of her bedroom she used her store of chiffon scarves and gloves, handed down to her by her glamorous Aunt, to perform her innocent version of the dance of the seven veils, which she had read about in some forgotten source. Unknown to the growing child, her sexuality was beginning to emerge aided by her imagination and obsession with pretty accessories.

Her imagination had been blamed for some terrifying nightmares. No other explanation accounted for the eight-year-old child's night terrors. Adult Rose found the solution out. Mum and Dad's quarrels became more and more vicious until on one occasion Dad declared that "Nothing in this house is yours." Saying this was like waving a red rag at a bull. Mum immediately got a part-time job in the canteen at a nearby colliery. There she met an older man, a mine foreman, who had time and money on his hands. He drove a Ford with the latest stylish tail fins and was himself a tall, handsome, grey-haired charmer. The car alone was something which Mum would have enjoyed. Rose now knew that this gentleman would come to the house when Dad was on night shift, throwing stones up at the bedroom window as a signal for Mum to go down and meet him for a drive. Rose realised that her young self might have known about this, and the nightmares were her involuntary physical, fearful reaction.

During this period of growing parental alienation, Mum must have been saving hard to develop her financial independence. She never missed work, so one bitterly cold winter morning she walked to the mine through unusually deep snow. This physical shock, it was thought, could have triggered the severe RA she began to suffer with when she finally was financially able to leave Dad. Much later, Mum explained more of her reasons for leaving. She told Rose about Dad's ideas with regard to girls' education. Like Victorian fathers, she alleged, he did not think girls should go to university, but should work, contribute money to the family and then marry and start their own families. Rose sometimes wondered how different her life would have been if she had been compelled to work in a factory at 15 years old. She certainly didn't want to start a family, given the example of Mum and Dad. So she counted her blessings. It seemed she had had a lucky escape as a result of Mum taking the dramatic step of marital separation. At least she had taken the children with her.

Of course, in retrospect Rose realised, Mary had her own Mum's example in her mind. Grandma had stayed with Grandpa until her children were all married, then left him. Why stay in your marriage when you find your life unbearable? But why go into marriage in the first place, Rose wondered? She vowed to herself that she would avoid that mistake. She would establish her own identity, using the agency she would develop through education, she promised her childhood self.

5

Teenage Years

AFTER CHRISTMAS 1961 Bill and Rose were removed from their schools and home and taken to Mum's rented house in a nearby town. The street was near the centre of town with a huge factory on the corner. Rose had no memory of the actual move but their new home was a semi-detached house with a back garden, a small kitchen and two living rooms on the ground floor, a coal cellar, two bedrooms and a bathroom on the first floor and an attic bedroom which became Rose's. Mum had done her best to make the children's new home appealing. Rose's room was freshly carpeted, and Mum had saved up enough to buy some new living room furniture: a snazzy black and yellow fur fabric lounge suite, an orange 'space rocket' standard lamp, and fibreglass curtains with a black and white bamboo design. Mum took the oldest bedroom suite and the children's beds from Dad's house as well as the piano, which had belonged to an older sister of hers. Rose's new room was spacious and light with a new bedroom suite, while Bill's small bedroom had some of the older furniture, as did Mum's. They had no TV and only a small fridge, with a leaking door seal.

Once they were settled in, Mum's seducer came to stay and life changed for the children. Sadly for Mum, life also changed for her. She began to suffer with RA very severely, and treated it with naturalist medications at first. Big bunches of herbs bubbling on the stove lent a strange smell to the house. It was obvious from inappropriate comments made after Mum had gone to bed early to ease her painful limbs that the new resident was not happy with the situation. He obviously had not planned to care for a sick lover, and probably was not ready to have another child at his advanced age either. It was unclear to Rose now how long he had stayed but he left after Mum became pregnant. There was no discussion of what had gone wrong. Nor had Rose been able to tell her mother what had been said to her. She had guessed she would not be believed and the predator had no doubt counted on that. Rose was extremely glad about the change in circumstances. She no longer had to withdraw to the safety of her own bedroom as soon as Mum went to bed early.

Both children went to the same school for the second term of the school year. Bill was in the first year, while Rose continued in the third year. It was a challenge for them both. However, Rose quickly found friends to make another foursome: Glenda, Jenny, and Caroline. Together they survived the school days, with occasional excitement such as the publication of the local literary hero, D.H. Lawrence's *Lady Chatterley's Lover.* No one knew where the copy had come from but it was passed around and groups of girls scoured the pages for 'dirty' words. It was obvious which group was reading the novel from the giggles and closeness of the heads together over the text. On weekends they were all in the school sports teams, hockey in winter and tennis in summer. In hockey Rose played the defence position of right back, feeling competent, but in tennis she was not as confident, only making the third pair. Still, sport was an interesting, new extension of her school life.

Sometimes on summer evenings she and Glenda would walk across town to a tennis club to improve their skills. It was good to have a friend to replace Angela who was now a 30 minute bus ride away. Many years later Rose ran into Angela, who related how she had cycled to town to visit Rose one day. Grandma had irrationally and hurtfully turned her away, saying Rose now had other friends. Rose had not been told of this. Glenda and Rose usually walked to and from school together. In summer they sometimes bought an apple from the greengrocer they passed on the way home. In those days there were plentiful varieties of apples: Cox's Orange Pippins, Worcester Permains, Golden Delicious, Granny Smiths. It was a treat to enjoy the juicy fruit as they wandered home. In winter they sometimes got together to listen to records on Glenda's Dansette. The two girls were happy in the front room. They were living the American dream, listening to Buddy Holly and drinking Nescafe, a recent introduction into British life, replacing the traditional cup of tea.

Mum had a new fulltime job in a cafe near the bus station and Rose began a Saturday job with her. She loved making Horlicks in the special pottery mug which had a smiling face wearing a nightcap on the rim. She also had to manage the dishwasher, which was a noisy, metal contraption, but as she was tall and strong, she managed it without complaint. She did not mind working, but at home she had to be in charge of Bill when Mum was at work, and this became a serious headache. Bill had his own friends at school, and he began to go train spotting, as their street was close to the railway line. He had to be up early to catch the 'fish', a special cargo train. He had one friend who was similarly fond of trains, and others who enjoyed playing football on the street. Unfortunately for Rose, he preferred both these pastimes to doing his homework and getting ready for bed in a timely manner. When Mum took on an additional job as a part-time evening barmaid, Rose's headache increased. Obviously Mum needed money to feed her two teenage children and the new baby. John was born a couple of years after the momentous move and Mum was his sole provider.

For Rose and Bill having a baby in the house was a new experience. Mum had a brief maternity leave, but then returned to work. She soon found another job which paid better and allowed her to give up the evening bar work which was impossible with a tiny baby to care for. Grandma came to live with them to help out, after Mum's lover went home to his wife. Sadly, one of Mum's brothers was outraged at her adultery, divorce and now the new child, so he took Grandma away. Luckily, the next-door neighbour, Aunty, became John's fulltime caregiver. Aunty was a part-time house cleaner for upmarket homes, and was able to take the toddler to work with her. These were strange years for all three children, but they coped. This was their life and they had to live it. Fortunately one of Mum's brothers was very kind, and often came round to visit with his wife. They had no children, so enjoyed taking the little family out in their Morris Minor to a nearby country park.

Living with a sole parent meant the children's

responsibilities had changed dramatically. They were latch key kids, supposed to look after themselves and of course, they started to become more independent as they made new friends. Rose still had the maternal instinct, however, bursting into tears when Bill broke his arm at school. "I'm the one who should be crying," he retorted scornfully when she was brought to see him in the Senior Teacher's office. Bill was a quiet, introspective child, with a strong independent streak. He had caused a few scares during his short life, including getting lost as a very young child on the beach in Southport, Lancashire. Then as a young teenager he travelled to Charing Cross for a day's train spotting when the family was holidaying in a caravan on the East Coast. He brought back a London evening newspaper to prove his exploit!

The change of schools had affected Rose more than Bill, she felt. They both left single sex schools for the same co-educational secondary school in the neighbouring county. The culture of the new school had been a shock for both children. Fortunately Bill had only missed one term of the curriculum, but Rose had not been able to make sense of the science and maths third year curriculum in the new school. Her young mind had been trained in General Science, then suddenly forced into Chemistry and Physics, with 'no parallax' as a kind of curse on her learning progress in science. Her achievement in maths suffered similarly, and she only managed to acquire the GCE qualification necessary for university entrance thanks to the extra tuition and kindness of a senior maths teacher. It had been terrifying for Rose to think that this one weakness, caused by the disruption of her school life, would prevent her from going to university.

Thanks to her kindly maths teacher she managed to get the 'O' level she needed. On the other hand, languages were her talent. She could learn them with ease, despite never having left England's shores until she was a Sixth Former.

Despite having given up her piano studies when she was 12, Rose continued to enjoy music. She became a member of the Bach Choir which practised on Wednesday evenings and performed in public occasionally. She relished singing big scores such as Handel's *Messiah*, and Mendelssohn's *Elijah*, standing in the contralto ranks with an older lady friend. As the school headmaster and his younger son were also in the Bach Choir a friendship began which progressed into 'boyfriend/girlfriend' status. They went on 'dates' to football matches, supporting the local team in the freezing cold, but holding hands well wrapped up was fun for a while. Rare parties given by older school students revealed to Rose the possibilities of girl/boy relationships, but given her family situation, the last thing Rose wanted was to end up with a baby. That was not going to be her ticket out of middle England, she knew well.

Rose's fifth year of school was memorable for several reasons, not just the birth of her baby brother. She made her first journey overseas to Austria on a two-week school trip led by the girls' sports teacher. It must have cost Mum an arm and a leg, and looking back Rose didn't know how she had managed it on her wages from the Singer Sewing Machine shop where she now worked, teaching clients how to use the sewing and knitting machines. Mum had made her some new clothes - a reversible anorak in green and yellow, the school colours, which Rose wore proudly with her brown, stretch polyester, ski pants, all the rage that season. The holiday had been thrilling, not simply because of being abroad, sleeping in a typical wooden mountain village chalet under a warm, fluffy, white duvet, and eating *bratwurst* and *nudelsuppe*, but on account of the slightly clandestine, much older, boyfriend she somehow acquired. Their sole 'date' had not been overly physical, but it had been highly charged. So much that Rose only realised she had lost her treasured medieval-style, leather, coin purse when she got back to her bedroom after curfew.

The headmaster's wife had put a stop to any further developments when the grapevine informed her that Rose had been out after dark. As Rose was dating the headmaster's younger son at the time back home, it had been rather indiscreet to even start this relationship. Nevertheless Klaus had been a penfriend for a while, despite Rose's near zero German and his minimal English. It had all ended, however, when Rose, with her lifelong personality traits of mistrust and sudden outbursts of fiery anger at any perceived hurt or insult, had felt she was being tricked after she noticed that Klaus' handwriting changed. She suspected someone was writing the letters for him, which in retrospect was understandable as he did not speak much English. However, she had written to end the relationship knowing that her forthcoming university studies as well as his age would prevent her from continuing the relationship further. On top of that, she had no money with which to travel, and neither did her parents, so the chance of seeing him again was potentially nil.

The relationship with the headmaster's son survived a little longer but Rose ended it when it became a little too hot to handle. As was the norm in those days, she then dated another schoolboy, who had pure blonde, smooth, shiny hair. This relationship centred on mutually enjoyed piano music and was short-lived, as Rose had tasted the *frisson* of sexual excitement and was not willing to put up with anything more placid. The next experiment was with a working young man, who expanded her horizons by taking her to a Notts. Forest football match in his car, but then expected more adult exploration within it. Rose had only been to Nottingham once before, to see John Neville in Shakespeare with a school group, so it felt like an exciting, grown-up date. This young man kept Rose company while babysitting for neighbours, even with a smelly sheep's head simmering on the stove to feed the resident greyhounds. He put up with the strong odour, no doubt hoping for some closer contact on the couch. But Rose's strong 'no premarital sex' principle compelled her to end the relationship quickly.

Meanwhile Mum was dismissed from her Singer job on account of her disability. She could not lift the heavy machines. Dismissal for this reason was not only heartless but against workers' and human rights by today's reckoning. She was compelled to move on to other jobs, trying to earn enough money to feed the family while her RA was increasing its painful impact on her body. She tried two factory positions, where her inability to stand and operate machinery was a disadvantage. She did all this without complaint, though it must have been very hard for her. She never told the children about her worries, struggling on stoically, despite her agony. Thankfully, later she was able to retrain for an office job in a new government-funded scheme.

Bill and Rose visited Dad every Sunday, after doing the

lunch dishes while listening to the comedy radio program *Round the Horn*. They walked across town to catch the bus to spend a couple of hours with Dad, returning with two sterling pounds each, for their 'keep'. Rose used to make a tinned salmon salad for their tea and the three would try to make conversation. The situation improved when Dad married his second wife. She was pretty, a good housekeeper, a wonderful cook and kind. She was blessed with her own child after a year of marriage. Mum had to struggle on suffering pain from more severely deteriorating joints. It was a hard life for her, and for her children, as they tried to assist her. It was worse for the baby, when the two older children completed school and escaped to university but Dad generously extended his financial maintenance contribution till both of his older children left school at 18.

6

Young Adulthood

IT STILL SURPRISED Rose that her Austrian escapade had not blackened her name at school. She was made Head Girl in her last year and also won the role of Little Buttercup in the school performance of Gilbert and Sullivan's *HMS Pinafore*. Although music was a minor talent in her youth, languages were Rose's forte. At her first secondary school she had excelled at Greek, Latin and French. French was Rose's major at university largely because there was no other 'living' language option in her new secondary school. She had been given the opportunity to study German for three months in the first year of the Sixth Form, and she had gained an A pass at 'O' level in this very short time. But there was no opportunity to study for 'A' level so she had to rely on her French, Latin and English Literature 'A' level results to get the grades she needed for university entrance. Having been successful, she took a summer job with Caroline at a holiday camp on the East Coast in order to earn some money before going to university in late September.

The seaside resort was popular for several reasons, but not the grey, North Sea which usually pounded the beach. On sunny days there were donkeys to ride and sandcastles to make, and on cold, windy days there were funfairs and amusement parks to entertain visiting families. The Miners' Welfare Assocation had established a holiday camp here which offered cheap accommodation and meals for miners and their families to take invigorating seaside holidays. *Skegness is so bracing*, was the logo. Billy Butlin, the millionaire entrepreneur, followed their example with a more upmarket version of the holiday camp. It had better chalets, offered babysitting, and the meals were more varied. There were also talent competitions and fun activities planned and guided by the famous Red Coats, the young people who had some talents themselves and who were expected to inject holiday fun where it was lacking. In the summer months many of the Red Coats were university students earning some holiday spending money. Waiters for the busy summertime were also recruited from school leavers and college students. Rose, Caroline and Caroline's boyfriend were waiters.

Rose could not remember Mum making any objection to her going away for the whole summer. She probably was glad to have one less mouth to feed and was probably more worried about the care of three-year-old John and her own worsening health. School had finished at the end of July, so 18-year-old Rose packed her bag, and caught the train with Caroline. They were billeted together in their own small chalet in a row which was dedicated to workers rather than holidaymakers. Uniform was a blue dress with a tight-fitting bodice, a full skirt and a white apron. Rose wore her own flat, black shoes, and her hair was tied back with a little white cap to facilitate hygienic meals service. She felt unattractive and unprepared for her work, but it didn't seem hard in theory. The duties were to serve breakfast, lunch and dinner to tables of 12 campers. To speed service up, there were racks which each held six plates filled with food. The waiting staff had to pick up two racks, walk as fast as possible to tables, offload the plates politely and collect them up again after the food was eaten. Campers stayed at the same table for a week, and if they had built up a rapport with their waiter, they gave a tip before they left. Tips were gratefully received, of course.

For the first week Rose felt clumsy and ill at ease, but gradually she settled into the routine and she had Caroline for company. However, after only a week, Caroline and her boyfriend began to quarrel. Things got worse until on the second weekend, Caroline stormed off home. Rose was left alone in a chalet, which wasn't acceptable to management and Rose didn't want to share with anyone else. So Rose was moved to the hostel for female staff. It was a blessing. She bunked with other girls she got on with very well, and was much happier than she had been before, wondering whether Caroline was coming back for the night or not.

The remaining weeks of the eight-week contract flew by. Rose didn't hear from Caroline but she was able to go out with some of the other girls who were university students. She enjoyed hearing from them about their studies. She even had a couple of dates. One night an older man invited her for a drink at a pub outside the camp. He was interesting, but too old for a teenager, so that was as far as it went. Another night a younger German, who spoke little English, asked her out. Remembering Klaus, Rose enjoyed the opportunity to practise her improved German but things got rather too hot for her to handle when she found herself in his chalet, trying to resist his ardent advances. After making her excuses and leaving she promised herself she would be more careful in future. She knew very well that sex before marriage could lead to inconvenient outcomes. Nor had it seemed very pleasant, so was not difficult to resist!

The last two weeks at the Camp were arduous. There was a shortage of staff and an increase in holidaymakers, so waiters were not given any days off. Rose remembered trekking backwards and forwards to the dining room to the sound of the Beatles *Yellow Submarine* playing over the tannoy system. She was getting more and more tired, and hotter and hotter during her hours of service. On the very last day of her contract, a Friday, salad was the normal evening meal. It was fortunate that it was a cold dish as Rose skidded on the damp floor and dropped both racks, a total of 12 meals. The holidaymakers applauded as they always did when there was an accident. "We're having a smashing time!" they shouted happily. Rose, her cheeks flushed with embarrassment, stoically went to pick up twelve more meals. She could hardly believe it when on her walk to the tables the same thing happened: She dropped both racks. It was too much: She could not continue her work, but ran out of the room sobbing. She had no idea how her tables were served after that. All she knew was that she would never do that job again. She had no tips for the week, but she didn't care. She was well out of it.

The next morning she took the train back home. She wore her best suit and felt happy and relieved to be going home. On the train a good-looking young man with dark, curly hair and a posh accent spoke to her. She was surprised at this interest but responded naturally to him. They chatted about their future studies, then, as she was about to get off the train, Paul gave her a card with his phone number on it. Rose had no home phone, but she promised to call him. As a result she went to his home town the following weekend. This visit was another eye opener. Paul lived with his parents in a large, detached house in a leafy suburb. His parents were elderly, and he was a quiet, shy person. They had little to talk about and not much opportunity for sexual adventure. She was not sure what he had in mind by asking her to visit, but she felt that her family's lowly social status did not make a good impression on his middle-class parents. The two of them visited Coventry Cathedral, rebuilt completely after WW2, went to a pub for a drink, and took walks in the rain, but the relationship was a non-starter.

Despite that disappointment, the comfortable house and rural environment gave Rose a standard of living to aspire to. Even though Paul had obviously been attracted to her, with her own low opinion of her bespectacled looks, Rose realised she would have to rely on her own efforts to leave the industrial town where she now lived. Her university education offered her a way out of the working-class, she realised, and she was determined to take it if she could. Her own efforts would be the method she preferred to utilise, since her experience of boyfriends so far had been rather disappointing, and marriage was certainly not on her agenda.

7

University, Year 1

AFTER THAT EVENTFUL working summer, Rose, with her school friends Gloria and Barbara set off from their Midlands town on the bus to Manchester University to study French Honours. Mum had been kind enough to go into a flurry of sewing, making new clothes, despite the increasing pain and disfiguration of her fingers, and of course, the limitations of Rose's summer vacation earnings. She had picked out some burgundy corduroy material and a contrasting shade of turquoise. Mum made a reversible, zipped jacket with a hood to withstand the North of England weather, and a burgundy miniskirt. She also made a paisley-patterned, burgundy corduroy mini-dress. It was lovely to have some new clothes for her new life. She still had to wear glasses, but there was more choice of frames for adults than for children, which was a consolation.

Rose was fortunate enough to receive a government grant for her studies. Both tuition and accommodation were provided for, thanks to the policies of the Labour Government of the day. During her first year away from home she was to live in 'digs', i.e. a boarding house, with seven other girls in the city's suburbs. She received a living and books allowance of ten pounds a week during term time only. During the holidays students were expected to be supported by their parents, or to work. Rose's degree program required her to spend the first summer holiday in France, so she decided to get a job during the year to save funds. She was lucky enough to get a Saturday job in a large department store in the centre of the city.

She enjoyed her work in the small administrative office. The staff members were kind to her and included her in their tea breaks and conversations. She spent most of her time on the attrition inventory, searching for and filing invoices for items that had got lost, stolen or damaged. The lady in charge of this duty fulltime was elderly, and guided Rose through the tasks in a pleasant manner. One day, on account of low staff availability Rose was summoned onto the shop floor to serve on the women's woollens counter. This was a delight for Rose, who had never had enough pretty or fashionable clothes in her life so far. She enjoyed folding sweaters which customers had unfolded, and searching the stock underneath the counter for a customer's specific needs. After an hour or so one particular customer attracted Rose's attention.

"Yes, Madam. Can I help you?" Rose asked.

The customer was tall, dark-haired, with strong facial features, well dressed, heavily made-up and equally heavily perfumed. She raised her left arm and jangled a charm bracelet in Rose's face. Rose, bemused, stared at the shiny, tinkling, gold tokens, and could make out a six-pointed star that had no significance for her at the time. She wondered what the customer wanted.

"You are one of us. I can help you." The customer declared, lowering her arm.

Rose continued to stare uncomprehendingly at the lady on the other side of the counter. She wondered if she would have to call security.

"Do you want me to help you?" the lady demanded, more forthrightly.

"No. No, thank you, Madam. It's very kind of you, but I'm fine." Rose stammered a polite response, without having the faintest idea that she had rejected support from one of God's Chosen People. Her own dark hair, dark eyes, and strong nose had perhaps given the customer the wrong impression of her religious background or ethnic origin.

A second incident brought the first into clearer focus and Rose began to understand the pros and cons of being a Jew in this big city. At lunchtime she liked to go window shopping and visit one of the other large stores. This particular day she was on the crowded escalator going down into the central City square, when she heard a clear, but nasty voice behind her saying,

"Go home. Get out of here. Clear off. Dirty Jew."

Rose was so surprised, she turned around to see who was speaking, and to whom. Higher up on the escalator, commanding a good view of the stairs, there was an old lady, bright eyes burning with a passion. The woman repeated her words loudly and clearly as she saw Rose turn. Rose flushed bright red. Although she wasn't a Jew, she understood in a lightning flash the hatred some felt for the race, and the vileness of anti-Semitism. Her political awakening could be attributed to that moment.

Rose's family was apolitical, she would have said, because

they never discussed politics. However, Dad belonged to the National Union of Mineworkers, and had given her Mao's *Little Red Book* and the *Communist Manifesto* when she was just a teenager. She had not read either text, so unaware was she of the political state of the nation or of the world. There was no one in her home environment who stood out from the white Anglo Saxon population. The only difference she had identified between people to this point in her life had been the influence of the Anglican and Catholic religions. Suddenly the world of the Jews had been revealed to her, in a personal way. She found it distasteful to recall both these incidents, but they stayed with her, as clear as day, as she recalled her younger life.

After experiencing the shame of those subjected to public venom, when a dark-skinned Indian student asked her to dance at a Students Union ball, she did not hesitate to accept. She had never spoken to a 'coloured' person before but she had no prejudice at all. The young man was clearly older as his hair was ever so slightly thinning, but he wore glasses as she did, he spoke very well, and he was a PhD student, something which even as a humble first year Arts undergraduate, she aspired to be herself one day. They began a steady relationship which stayed platonic as Rose was sticking to her personal code of conduct. These were the days prior to the availability of the contraceptive pill. Rose knew that sex was a potential trap, which could not therefore be experienced before marriage. Rose smiled as she recalled the first time she had gone to visit Ramadas in his small flat for Sunday lunch. He had met her at the bus stop, waiting there a long time as he did not want to miss her bus. A police patrol car had stopped and questioned him to his bemusement. When Rose finally arrived she found him upset at the attitude of the policemen as well as grey-faced with cold.

As a PhD student from a good family in India, Ramadas was paying high fees to study in this chilly northern atmosphere. He had regained his normal high spirits as they walked back to his place, and he prepared the strangest meal she had ever eaten, though she did not say so. He proudly presented a plate with a mini pork pie and a large spoonful of canned marrowfat peas. He had been afraid to offer Rose a curry, so had invented a meal which he hoped she would like. Another time he showed how he, a boy who had always had servants, had taught himself Indian cuisine. He prepared fish fingers in a mustard curry sauce, with mashed potatoes. Both these dishes were perfectly edible to a girl living on a student budget in digs.

Marie from North East England was Rose's roommate in digs. An only child, she had not lived away from her mother's tender care before and did not even know how to wash a jumper, she confessed. Despite the differences in their upbringing and their lifestyles the two became firm friends. Rose laughed a lot at Marie's different ways. She was a pretty, trim, petite young woman with a vivacious smile, a pert nose and apparently, waist-length fair hair. Boys flocked around her, especially on her Geography major courses where girls were in the minority. The two girls' social circles rarely crossed. Marie thought nothing of staying over at a boyfriend's house, taking off her luxurious long wig and placing it on the bedpost overnight, amazing the sleeping young man with her short crop in the morning. Like Rose, Marie loved food, and Friday nights were always memorable when the house 'father' cooked fish and chips, with braised celery as a delicious side vegetable. For the eight girls seated around the large oval table, dinner time was lovely, with the fragrant smell of the food, which disappeared in far too short a time. Marie's face would fall as she realised the meal was at an end. "That went down so well," she would say, scraping her plate clean.

In the first week at university Rose had joined the Gilbert and Sullivan Club and the University Choir. The Club members performed a musical once a year, and to her surprise, Rose was asked to audition for the housekeeper role in the *Tower Warders*, which required a contralto solo. Rehearsals took place once a week and the performance was a success. The only concern for Rose was that she was made up to look old, and some of her teeth were blacked out. (The vinyl recording of that performance was later destroyed in the invasion of Kuwait.) As for the Choir, she enjoyed taking part in a performance of *Messiah*, which she already knew. With a job, a new boyfriend and her studies there was no time for any other leisure commitments.

It was a requirement of Rose's four year Bachelor's degree program that students spent at least one year in France. This was arranged by the Department and built into the third year of the degree, but undergraduates were also encouraged to spend summer vacations in France. As Gloria had not visited France either, the two friends signed up for a Christian working holiday in the South of France after their first year of study. It was an exciting prospect. They had eight weeks of work with accommodation and food provided but no pay. Afterwards they planned to spend at least a week hitch-hiking around the Midi region. Hitch-hiking was a cheap method of travel common and not so dangerous in the 1960s. They took a tent so that they would be able to camp overnight, spending as little money as possible. With no paying holiday job they needed to watch their budget.

On arrival in the work camp Rose was lucky enough to find a little job in the village looking after two small children in the mornings and babysitting at weekends to help out their *Parisienne* mother, who was holidaying alone and in need of a rest. With the limited experience of caring for her much younger brother, Rose enjoyed preparing bowls of hot chocolate with slices of toasted brioche for breakfast and playing games with them. The very young children found her French accent amusing, but they were not badly behaved, so it was a fun experience. The international group of young 'workers' were also interesting. They took it in turns to cook in pairs for the rest of the group. Gloria and Rose were dumbfounded to be faced with rabbits as the main ingredient in the evening meal they had to prepare. Fortunately breakfast was easier, and lunch was sandwiches. In their working hours they were building terraces on the steep slopes of the *Alpes Maritimes*, but in their rest time they could sunbathe and enjoy the local environment. On one occasion they walked to an area where ammonites could be found. Although Rose could not identify any, a young man offered her a lovely specimen which she still had on her bookshelf.

When Rose got back to the UK she had lost a lot of weight and was very tanned. She had enjoyed her time in France and had not found herself another love interest, despite a close encounter in a campsite in Frejus. The girls had pitched their tent successfully after an initial struggle with a stone as they had forgotten to bring a hammer to use on the tent stakes. The neighbour with a hammer in the next tent was an attractive young man from Austria, reminding Rose of her brief dalliance with Klaus. After loaning his hammer, this young man invited the girls for a drink with him, but Gloria declined. Rose felt it would be rude not to accept as they were not planning to go out. As dusk fell and after a couple of drinks and a chat in German/English the atmosphere in the tent was getting warmer but as Rose enjoyed a tentative embrace, she heard the sound of sobbing from the girls' tent. Either Gloria was homesick, lonely or afraid of what might happen next. Apologetically and hastily Rose made her excuses and left. She had not corresponded with the young man afterwards, though they had exchanged addresses.

On another occasion Rose was lucky to come through unscathed: A taxi driver who picked them up and drove them to a campsite seemed to expect 'payment in kind' and insisted on driving one of them up to a lonely, but beautiful viewpoint. Rose realised Gloria could not cope with this, so she agreed to go with him. Fortunately she was clearly naive as well as not fluent in French, so the man, after offering her a cigarette and a drink, both of which she refused, and then attempting a conversation which Rose pretended not to understand, drove her intact back to the campsite.

The people whose lifts they accepted seemed above board except for one large auto with four rather seedy-looking blokes who stopped near Draguignan. As the two girls had been waiting a long time and the day was drawing on, they reluctantly accepted the lift but felt grateful to emerge unharmed near Grasse. The '60s was still an age of innocence for many women, despite the new focus on sex and 'free love'. The two girls had enjoyed the summer, and their French had definitely improved. The second year of university awaited them on their return to the UK.

8
University, Year 2

DURING ROSE'S SECOND year she and Ramadas moved into the same house but rented separate bedsitters. Mum made curtains and a matching bedspread in Rose's favourite colours, blue and gold, for her tiny room, which became her dressing room and walk-in-wardrobe. On weekdays Rose had to attend lectures, whereas Ramadas was working in the University Library all day and every day, completing revisions on his English Literature PhD thesis. They developed a routine of meeting in the Library at the end of the day and travelling on the bus home together. Ramadas taught Rose to make simple Indian curry dishes, and snacks such as *pakora*, served with plain yoghurt and mint. They often ended meals with comfort food, such as ginger loaf with warm custard. On Saturdays after work in the store Rose would join Ramadas in the Central Library, an imposing round building in the City centre. Together they would go shopping for takeaway food or have a drink and a snack in the Students Union. On Sundays they took a walk in the park and continued with their studies. Life was orderly and satisfying; Rose felt understood and unpressured. Their chaste relationship lasted for two years.

Ramadas had a few close friends among the Indian and Pakistani Students Club but mostly they kept to themselves and their studious routine. As well as completing her own reading and written assignments for Latin, Italian and French, Rose edited the final submission of Ramadas' PhD thesis that year. One weekend they broke their routine and took a trip on the National Coachline down to London where Ramadas needed to visit the British Museum Reading Room. It was exciting for Rose to see this high precinct of academe. As neither of them had much money they stayed in the Holland Park Youth Hostels Association and did not indulge in luxuries. It was a proud day when Ramadas received his doctoral degree at the end of Rose's second year. Ramadas had bought Rose an early birthday present to thank her for her endeavours. She wore the fashionable, beige, three-quarter-length, suede coat he had given her for his graduation ceremony. Looking back, Rose realised now that this was the only graduation she attended. Despite gaining two BAs, one MA and an Ed.D herself, she was never able to attend her own ceremonies.

After graduating, Ramadas was due to take up a position as a lecturer in English in a college in his home state. Presumably he had to recompense his parents for the overseas student fees they had paid for him. He seemed happy to be leaving, so Rose was surprised when he asked her to marry him and go to India with him. He had visited her home and met her Mum and younger brother, so he was under no illusion about her working-class status. But Rose was to spend the following year in France as an English language teaching assistant and despite her attachment to him she considered herself too young to settle down before she was even 21. She had her own dreams of independence and was not interested in giving up on them. When she gently let him down, he seemed to understand her position. As they said their goodbyes, they both promised to write and packed up to move to the next stage of their careers.

9

Year 3, in Provence

ROSE'S SUMMER HOLIDAY was spent at home, where Mum needed her to look after John while she trialled gold injection treatments for her severe RA. It was a stressful time. Mum was hospitalised 30 miles from home and visiting was slow and difficult on public transport. On her first visit Rose hoped to hide the fact that John was missing his Mum and had a fever. But Mum guessed at the truth, immediately discharged herself and came home with Rose. This was the second time Mum had turned down the opportunity to trial a new treatment. The first had been at a hospital appointment during the onset of RA when another female patient warned her against having cortisone injections. This treatment was not effective, and later gold was also proven of no help. So John's fever intervened at the right time.

The rest of summer was spent preparing to teach in France for an entire school year. Rose would receive a salary and Mum once again made some new clothes for her. Using one pattern made up in two different materials, she made a blue and white gingham, short, frilled wrap *a la Brigitte Bardot* and a long, red, brushed nylon dressing gown. The gingham matched Rose's bikini so became beachwear. Both garments lasted many years as Rose, accustomed to being frugal, took great care of her clothes. Even now she would divide the cost of the item by the number of 'wears' to work out if a garment could go in the rag bag!

Rose turned 21 in the South of France. It was a lonely birthday at the end of September, made worse since the weather seemed cold and bleak, even in this warm region of France. Having arrived in town on the weekend before classes began, Rose was staying in a small hotel while she looked for a more permanent place to live for the school year. Her birthday fell on Saturday and there happened to be a wedding party in the hotel. Rose was living on sandwiches, snacks and tinned food, so it was bittersweet to see the lavish *croquembouche* wedding cake standing on the huge oak dining table as she went up to her little room that evening. There was no one to talk to and Mum had no phone. Rose shed some solitary tears that night, but knowing that life was hard she had to be brave. After all, she was living in France and on her way to achieving her degree. And she had her health.

A visit to the *Mairie* (townhall) the following Monday raised hopes of a cosy home. She was told: "There's an old lady who lives alone. She has a nice sun *terrasse* too." Rose went round to see the house and the old lady agreed a price for the one room she could rent out. It was small but adequate, though Rose noted heating was supplied by a solitary burner in the centre of Madame's living room. Winter was approaching, and Rose wondered aloud about the need for heating in her own bedroom. The old lady assured her:

"If we leave your door open, then your room will be warm."

Of course that meant there would be no privacy but Rose was feeling in need of company, so she didn't worry about that. The month of October passed quickly. Rose ate lunch at school with the other *professeurs*. School lunch was a delicious, cooked meal, bigger than Rose was used to eating in her student days. She relished the Provencal cuisine with beautiful stuffed tomatoes, peppers stewed with olives and risottos, pastas and *'patates' dauphinoises*. She slowly got to know one or two of the teachers better. They all had busy lives. The one who became closest to Rose was Brigitte, a petite blonde with waist-length hair and large brown eyes. She dressed very smartly and had a small son named Jean. Brigitte helped her settle in and one day invited her to come for tea after school. The two young women walked to the primary school to collect Jean. He munched on a slice of crusty fresh baguette with two squares of chocolate pressed into the *mie*, or crumb, as they continued on towards home. Brigitte lived in a huge, stone-built house. The ceilings were high and the rooms echoed with their voices, but rather strangely, also rang out with hammer blows.

"Ah, le gosse, il s'occupe a casser les murs!" Brigitte shouted. *"Il me fait mal a la tete!"*

Rose was amazed to see that the five-year-old was indeed hammering away at the thick walls in a corner of the sitting room, without impunity, other than his mother shouting at him to make less noise.

"Oh, *les francais*," she thought. "If we'd done that at home it would have been punishment and then bedtime!"

A routine was established with Brigitte after school, so

Rose spent very little time other than sleeping at Madame's house. On sunny Sundays she was sometimes invited to sit on the terrace under the grapevine in the sun, from where Madame would call out to her neighbours in a piercing voice: *"Cou cou, ne ne!"*

This was repeated several times, until another voice replied: *"Cou cou!"*

"Ca va?"

"Oui ca va tres bien, merci."

A conversation would then ensue in broad *langue d'oc,* the original Provencal language.

Meanwhile Gloria had settled into a more welcoming and comfortable family situation in her placement in St. Etienne. She encouraged Rose to visit her for the upcoming *Toussaint* All Saints' Holiday, a long weekend. Rose bought a train ticket, but did not book a seat, unaware that there would be standing room only on such a busy weekend. It was not too bad on the way north, but returning after a happy time with Gloria, the train was overcrowded, the corridors were packed with people standing, and worst of all, the weather took an unexpected turn for the worse: It began to snow, a rare phenomenon in Provence. When Rose got back to the house, frozen and tired from the long journey, she found her bedroom glacial. Madame had kept her door firmly closed over the weekend and there was no way Rose could warm up, even after a hot shower. Tears again fell on her pillowslip, but this time Rose decided she had had enough. If the winter was going to be harsh, she could not stay there.

After a poor night's sleep Rose went into school next day and told Brigitte and the other teachers about her problem.

They were all shocked and willing to help. By the end of the day another home had been found *chez* an elderly couple who were wealthy farmers. They had a large house in town with a small apartment attached for their daughter to use when she came down from Paris, which was rarely. One of the teachers came round to the old lady's house and explained the problem Rose was having. She moved out the same day and was welcomed into the warmth of the elderly couple's home. The new apartment had just two rooms but they were a palace after the small, cold bedroom which had been home to Rose till then. There was a large bedroom with a comfortable double bed, much more opulent than the narrow, single, steel-sprung bed in her first 'home' and a large dining kitchen which had double doors giving onto a farmyard, with a huge glass and metal aviary on the left hand side. Sunlight and birdsong filled this entrance, so breakfasting felt like a special experience. Rose told Gloria she must come down to visit as soon as possible.

There was a private entrance into the apartment from the interior of the huge house. This door had a giant-sized key, and one handle which needed to be transferred to the outside when leaving, then pocketed with the key. It made for a slow exit until Rose got used to it. Internally there was an adjoining door into the couple's home from the bedroom, which gave onto a lovely corridor with a couple of lemon trees already flowering in autumn in pots. The elderly couple seemed to enjoy having Rose around, inviting her into their home each evening to watch the *actualites*. It was wonderful to feel relaxed after the tension of October. Rose began to feel more settled and was able to enjoy her work and make a few friends.

Staff in the school were used to welcoming an *assistante anglaise*, so she was invited to dinner one evening by the senior English teacher. It was cosy in his small family home in the centre of town, close to the *Centre LeClerc* where Rose did her food shopping. The school secretary also invited her for lunch with her family one Saturday. Rose felt adventurous as she took the bus to the nearby small town. It was very interesting to see how different people lived. Madame school secretary had a sunny modern villa on the outskirts of town. She also had an interesting back story. She had lived in Algeria before the War of Independence, and referred to herself as a Pied Noir. Rose understood, despite her lack of knowledge of this war, that the French residents of Algeria who had fled the fighting were called *Pieds Noirs* by those living in mainland France. Rose did not know enough French to comment on this difficult political topic, so hoped she did not come over as uncaring. Having to leave one's home on account of war seemed horrific, and she hoped her sympathy showed.

Another young teacher invited her to have dinner in her small town centre apartment one day. This taste of her life suggested that Stephanie seemed to be living the kind of free, single life that Rose aspired to. One day out of the blue a teacher from another school, the more academic *lycee* in Avignon, came by and invited her to visit on a weekend. Her cottage-style home in the countryside was what Rose hoped she might be able to own one day. Travelling there through the fields covered with rotting apples which were not picked because there was no profit in it, seemed both sad and yet thrilling to Rose. She was finally living a different life, an exciting one. An opportunity also came up for excitement of a different kind. A young, attractive, male teacher offered to take her to the naturist beach on the Mediterranean, an hour or so drive away. With no regret Rose turned the offer down.

More suitable and fun was a weekend meeting in Avignon of the teaching assistants in the area, where Rose was pleased to meet colleagues. On other weekends Rose occupied herself with short solo forays into the region, such as visiting the setting for the novel *Tartarin de Tarascon*, with Alphonse Daudet's writing in her mind. Van Gogh's history in Provence was inspiring and Aix en Provence's ancient architecture was lovely. Her hosts introduced her to modern architecture by Balladur and Le Corbusier, driving her along the coast to see the apartments each had constructed. Also, on Wednesday afternoons when school was closed she began to attend the University in Marseille where Brigitte was studying for a teaching diploma.

The Christmas holiday was short but Rose travelled back by train to see her Mum and brothers. She was still experiencing the lower abdominal pain she had often felt during her second year at university. Visiting her local doctor she was given some kaolin and morphine tablets to keep the pain under control. Once back for the Spring Term in France, however, she became much sicker and was unable to eat at all. The elderly couple were very concerned, even grilling a *biftek de cheval* to tempt her appetite. This was enough to finally confirm Rose as a vegetarian. She was so thin by now she was nicknamed the English string, *la ficelle anglaise*. After several inconclusive investigations the surgeon, a big burly man in a white coat, adored by the bevy of pretty female nurses in his local clinic, decided to operate on 14 February, Valentine's Day.

Rose had been receiving letters from Ramadas until Christmas but since New Year she had not had any communication from him. She had not paid much attention as her health was occupying her thoughts. So it was a surprise to be given an airmail envelope by the nurse who administered her premed. injection. In a slightly dazed state she stared at the envelope. She did not recognise the handwriting. Tearing it open she read the tragic news. Ramadas had been in a head-on car crash while travelling to his college in the Himalayan foothills above Patna. He was brain-damaged. Rose screamed and then burst into tears. She was suffering from shock and the sedation was taking effect. It was not until several days later that she was able to pick up the letter again.

Once she was on the operating table and after searching deep into her lower abdomen, the surgeon finally found a severely abscessed appendix. The operation took hours and Rose was in excruciating pain that night. A nurse was posted to stay by her side. The nurse told her the next day that she had spoken French, saying she wanted to die. Rose was bedridden for a month afterwards, needing a drain in the incision for most of that time. Mum turned grey overnight when *M. le Principal* wrote a letter in French, saying her daughter was gravely ill and needed to be visited. Mum had to send the letter to John's primary school for translation. Meanwhile Rose had managed to alert Gloria to her predicament. She generously came and stayed in the apartment, visiting Rose each day. She even cooked rice pudding for her!

Other visitors were bringing in *langues de chat, calissons d'Aix*, a local marzipan specialty, and *madelaines,* but Rose didn't feel up to eating much, though she enjoyed the Clinic's spinach *a la creme*. Mum in the UK could do nothing to help, with no money, a job to hold down, and a small child to look after, but brother Bill came to the rescue. He hitch-hiked down to Avignon, sleeping overnight in hedgerows, and was able to go on holiday with Rose for a recuperative trip. This was the best gift of all, and Rose was very grateful to him.

Neither Rose nor Bill had much money, so together they hitchhiked into Spain with a Portuguese dancer who had been working in Germany. She drove her little Volkswagen like a madwoman and they were stopped at least twice by traffic police on the *autoroute* into Spain. Once they had reached Barcelona the three of them slept in a cheap dormitory, then the English pair made their excuses and stayed put, rather than continuing into Portugal. After sightseeing in Barcelona they hitch-hiked out of the city to the suburb of Badalona. Here they found a cheap hotel for a night, then an even cheaper backpacker's where they stayed for a few days enjoying the sunshine. These were the restricted times of General Franco's dictatorship, when Spanish students were keen to practise their English with visitors. So one afternoon they spent sipping *sangria* and conducting English conversation in a private house. Bill swore that the boys were hoping for a little more fun, but Rose felt they had excitement enough just talking and drinking wine.

Hitch-hiking out of Spain back to Provence was not so easy, but eventually they found a lorry driver who would take them and their string bag - all the luggage they had with them! After a night to recuperate, Rose took Bill into Avignon for a last meal. He ordered a steak which was so rare it had to be returned several times to the kitchen until he was able to eat it. Rose knew for sure that she was vegetarian! She saw Bill off on the night-sleeper train back to Paris, where he took the train/hovercraft back to the UK. At least she had been able to pay for his return journey. It had been great fun to spend this time together. Rose had never forgotten it.

Of course, having recuperated to some extent, Rose had to deal with the issue of Ramadas' accident and status. She wrote to his uncle and explained her situation. She was young, she was still a student with no savings, and although she was very sorry about the tragedy, she did not want to give Ramadas hope that they would be together. She felt that she could not continue writing to him as his uncle said he recognised her letters. So it would be worse to make him think she would be coming to his rescue. An instinct of self-preservation helped her make this decision, but for the rest of her life India held a special place in her heart.

The rest of the school year was uneventful apart from a friendship built up with Josephine, a senior student at the school who was a sweet-natured, sensible, studious girl. She invited Rose to Sunday lunch with her family. Josephine's parents were very welcoming though they spoke no English at all, so Rose was compelled to use her own language skills. All in all the teaching year had been a success, despite the serious illness and time spent in hospital. She expected to stay in touch with Brigitte in the future, but made no promises.

When Rose got back home Mum was relieved to see her, after the serious operation she had had in February. Rose was saddened to see that Mum's hair had turned white as a result of the shock the Principal's letter had given her. Rose did her best to look after Mum, giving her hot baths and taking over the shopping, cooking and cleaning. She even did some spring-cleaning and painted the pantry and kitchen. She enjoyed seeing her little brother John, now a lively six-year-old, with his own bright personality seemingly unaffected by his life with a disabled single parent. He now had a little cat, called *Minou* with a nod to the French, and loved it dearly, though he'd had some difficulty persuading Mum to accept this pet after her earlier disaster with the little dog.

10

University, Final Year and Camp America

AFTER HER YEAR abroad Rose felt more confident as she took her place back at university for her final year of study for her BA Honours degree, despite having nowhere to live. She went to the University Accommodation Office to enquire about bedsitters. Then, in the first lecture she met up with a petite young woman with huge blue eyes. Suzanne was a little older and much more mature than Rose. She had already found herself a flat in the house of a University Lecturer in Wythenshawe. She needed a flatmate, *et voila*, the problem was solved. The girls each had a bedroom with a shared bathroom and tiny kitchen.

There was no living room so when they wanted to give dinner parties, or lunches, using Rose's Indian culinary arts, they spread the buffet on low tables in Suzanne's huge room and sat on floor cushions to eat. Bill had come to their rescue with a saw, cutting the legs off wash-stands they had bought cheaply from the Salvation Army and then painted white. With floor cushions and large, white, paper lampshades, in typical Bohemian student style, the effect was casual and relaxed. Mary and Abdul, a couple of Ramadas' friends from Rose's second year, were now married. Rose visited them in their home and they came over for one of the famous curry lunches. They were saddened to hear about Ramadas, but there was little anyone could do other than sympathise and berate life's unfairness. *Ceuillez des aujourd'hui les roses de la vie* was the apt Ronsardian philosopy.

Both Rose and Suzanne had a lot of work to do in their final year as each had a thesis to write. Rose chose to research Gaston de Foix, a medieval knight in the South West of France. Froissart and Joinville de Villehardouin were her source texts. She enjoyed returning to the Library stacks, staying there for long hours as she had done with Ramadas and digging out the information she needed. She had hoped to type her own manuscript so attended public evening classes at a local secondary school where she made some female friends. But her typing skills were not strong enough so she paid a professional typist to do the job. On completion, her thesis was submitted to an external examiner, a professor in Glasgow University, which meant she had to travel to Scotland for the very first time, for a *viva voce*. The trip was a vague memory, but she passed. In spite of the hours of study preparing for final exams as well as completing the thesis, Rose had several friendships on the go.

Rose's diaries suggest she was spinning like a top in her free time! She met another postgraduate Indian student, nearer her own age, with whom she kept up the social contact with the Indian and Pakistani Student Clubs. This young man gave her a beautiful, silk chiffon sari which she eventually passed on to Suzanne, who was keen to wear it. With some of the young secretaries from evening class she went to nightclubs. Rose loved dancing and frequently stayed out till the early hours of the morning. One of those nights she met a young Malaysian student of accounting, very good-looking, shy and gentle. Their relationship included dancing and visits to weekly plays, concerts and films. Rose was burning the student candle at both ends in this, her final year.

Another brief but eventful friendship began in a nightclub. Alan was a young businessman who invited her to a party at his home. It was winter and it had snowed, so Rose put on her prized purchase of an antique fox stole, over her party dress. The party was a family affair, quite boring really, until Rose accepted a glass of home-made beer from Alan's father. That was the last she remembered until waking up the next day, thankfully in her own bed. Suzanne explained how she'd come home in a taxi, collapsed on the front door, and vomited violently once she got upstairs. Suzanne had undressed her and put her to bed. Reviewing the clothes she had worn, Rose quickly realised that her fur stole was not there. A phone call to Alan, who went searching for it, revealed that she had dropped it outside and it had been left in the snow, driven over by other guests' cars. Rose was so angry she refused to see Alan again! Now, of course, Rose would never wear real fur.

Sickness was the start of a friendship on another occasion after Rose bought pike from a local butcher's shop on the road to university. As Rose didn't eat meat, she rarely looked in the butcher's window, but one evening she noticed a sign saying 'Fresh Pike'. Writhing in agony after eating it that night, Rose was given morphine to ease the intestinal pain of food poisoning. The next time she walked to University she went into the shop and complained. The owner offered to take her out for dinner as an apology. Rose demurred but gave in when he said he would take her to a top restaurant favoured by famous footballers. That night she enjoyed the special occasion. Although the older man was married, he was separated, so there were some pleasant evenings at the theatre followed by excellent dinners. Any boyfriend who tried to persuade her to abandon her 'no sex before marriage' principle was defeated but this more experienced lover taught her some tricks which did not impinge on her virtue and which anyone who bought Cosmopolitan magazine could read about, with graphics provided. The '60s were moving sex into the mainstream media. Masters and Johnson's research was becoming well known and *The Joy of Sex* was a best-seller.

This final year of social events and study passed too quickly and exams were looming. Mindful of the future, Rose went to see the Careers Advisors to discuss her prospects. She would have liked to continue her studies with a Master's degree but that was out of the question as there was no funding available for research. A languages degree had prepared her for a choice of three careers: teaching, secretarial work, or the armed forces. Rose had hoped to be an interpreter but French and German were both necessary. A secretarial diploma with translating skills was the next best thing, and it could be government-funded. So Rose enrolled for a fourth study year, at a polytechnic in London, a city she knew only a little. In addition, she applied to be a counsellor in the Camp America Summer Camp program. In exchange for work, accommodation and food were free, but the charter return airline ticket cost 60 pounds sterling. Once again Bill came to the rescue, lending her the money she would pay back with the coming year's study grant. After farewells to the family in June she flew to the USA from Gatwick, with other international camp counsellors.

Rose was to work in a Girl Scout Camp in Upstate New York, in a forest near a lake. She was pleased to find there were two Danish counsellors at the same camp. Rose was placed with the youngest Girl Scouts, accommodated in large tents which slept six people. The counsellors all stayed in the same tent and had a duty rota for night time when they were required to accompany their young charges to the bathroom. Rose made everyone laugh by referring to the flashlight they needed on this precarious journey, as a torch, which conjured up an image of the Olympic flame. Racoons and chipmunks could enter the tent both day and night, so food was forbidden in the tent. Meals were served in a large canteen which did double duty as a meeting place and activity hall when it rained. Outdoor activities included games, sports, hiking and swimming in the lake. American Independence Day was celebrated with a BBQ of hotdogs, and a serious attempt to throw the only UK Camp Counsellor into the lake. In the evenings, campfires, toasted marshmallows and 'S'mores' were accompanied by international folk songs, many of which Rose could still sing: *Chevaliers de la table ronde*, *Il Partigiano*, *Kumbaya*, and Joan Baez's *Donna Donna* and *We shall overcome*, as well as Bob Dylan's *Blowing in the Wind*. The '70s was the decade of student revolt against the Establishment, and the search for Peace and Love instead of War.

Rose was befriended by two American counsellors

and invited to stay in their homes on their occasional free weekends. Eve's family was third-generation Italian. Her Dad gave Rose a baseball bat and a beer glass shaped like a hyacinth bowl. For years afterwards Rose drank beer only from that special glass, while baby brother John took ownership of the baseball bat as his late-night bus-driving defensive weapon. Bunty's family had a beautiful home and to Rose's amazement, Bunty gave a party at which most of the students smoked marijuana. Rose could hardly believe her eyes, seeing party guests talking to themselves or laughing at nothing. Nothing would persuade Rose then or later to take drugs. It seemed so pointless. Bunty was a photographic artist. She sent several black and white photos to Rose and later visited London. But the friendship faded after Bunty married and had a daughter. As in France, friendships enriched Rose's stay in the USA. She had dared to exist in very different communities from the one she had been brought up in. The constraints of her childhood would not limit her future, it seemed. The world was indeed now her oyster.

Then came the cherry on her Camp America cake: Her maternal aunt and uncle invited her to fly to California to stay with them in San Francisco. They bought a return ticket East to West Coast for her so it was an invitation she could not refuse, even though she had never met this Aunt, one of Mum's older sisters. Evelyn had emigrated after WW2 with her husband, Rob, and had her only child in California. Cousin Marion was older than Rose, and married with three children. Rose had seen photos of them all in Mum's album and she looked forward to meeting them. The modern, attractive bungalow her aunt and uncle lived in delighted her. They had a swimming pool and peach trees from which she picked her own breakfast. It was an idyllic vision of what life could be like if you worked hard and took advantage of life's opportunities. They visited Reno in Nevada, ate on Fisherman's Wharf in San Francisco, walked on the Golden Gate Bridge, visited the Redwood Forest, and went to Disneyland. Compared to the standard of living in 1960s Britain, even the fridge was 'out of this world' so Rose came home to the UK with a new, if materialistic, conception of a possible future.

11

Postgraduate Diploma

ON RETURNING TO the UK at the end of September Rose faced financial minimalism. She had already found somewhere to live, having made contact with Marie, her old room-mate from first year university. They shared a bedsitter in Clapham which was handy for the station and buses to Victoria but far from College. The rent was cheap for London and Rose had received her grant for accommodation, living and books for the first term of her Postgraduate Secretarial Diploma, but she needed to pay back the money borrowed from her brother. Bill was now in his last year at university, studying politics and economics, and needed his cash back. After fulfilling her promise Rose then had the sum of one shilling per day for food. (Decimal currency, or 'new money', came in later that year.) As her course was not academic, she was hoping to get away without purchasing books for the first term at least.

Sharing a flat with Marie was easy because she hardly saw her. Their working hours were diametrically opposed: Marie worked from late evening to early morning, usually crossing paths with Rose as she left in the early morning to go to college till early evening. Marie had completed her geography degree more than a year ago, and after that a teaching diploma but had chosen not to go into the profession. Instead, she was working as a hostess at a London club, where she was hired to chat to clients, encourage them to order fake champagne at exorbitant prices for her to drink, and to buy her expensive boxes of cigarettes. This generated profits for the club and Marie earned a percentage of the takings. As she could take home the boxes of 200 cigarettes and she was not a smoker, she could sell them for extra income. As luck would have it, Rose soon found steady customers for the cheap tobacco.

Rose had been subsisting for a month on a diet of two pounds of carrots or two pounds of apples per day, priced at one shilling, from a market stall near college. She was beginning to feel the strain of such a restricted diet, so decided to get a part-time job. Leaving college to attend an interview for a barmaid at a pub at the far end of the King's Road, she almost ran into a tall, bespectacled man. He seemed confused as the door was not signposted for entry or exit to the College, so Rose asked a fateful question:

"Can I help you?"

The man took the opening gambit, turned right around and accompanied her to the Underground Station, chatting all the way. Rose found his banter unusual: He asked if she would teach him French, when his distinctive accent suggested he was French. For her pub interview she was wearing her burgundy corduroy mini-dress, with Marie's Baker's Boy burgundy velvet hat and Charles Jourdan patent leather shoes. Twiggy was the idol of the time and Rose had maintained her own thin frame thanks to a period of anorexia, then bouts of compulsive eating and bulimia starting in her final University year. Also, she had paid for tinted lenses in her spectacles to prevent fluorescent light-triggered migraines with a secondary aim of making the thick lenses less noticeable. So she felt confident in her appearance, and noted with approval her companion's trendy leather jacket with a small, knotted silk scarf at his neck. His hair was longish and wavy, his complexion fair and he had the *panache* of a bohemian Frenchman.

They entered the Tube Station and the Circle/District lines together but travelled towards their destinations in opposite directions, Rose towards Sloane Square, her companion towards Gloucester Road. As they parted the man thrust a coin and a piece of paper into Rose's hand. She looked at the sixpenny piece and the name and number on the paper in amazement.

"That's so you can call me," he said. "I know I can't call you, but you can't avoid calling me now."

Rose laughed. Obviously she had made an impression on him, though she was more focussed on the upcoming interview than on calling this stranger. To her pleasure Rose got the pub job and started work the next day. She could work two or three weekday evenings.

The following Monday the young man she had met came back to College. She recognized him at once in the huge restaurant at coffee break. He rose and greeted her.

"Do you remember asking me if you could help me?"

"Yes," she murmured. "So what?"

"Well you can help me by having lunch with me. There's a pub nearby, which is typically English. I think it's called The Bishop. What time do you finish for lunch?"

"At 12.45. But I've only got an hour."

"OK, that's fine. I'll meet you here. It's only five minutes' walk away."

Rose agreed to meet him and returned to her lectures. At lunchtime she found him waiting for her at the main exit. She had never been in the pub before. It was rather upmarket and the decor was impressive with panelled oak walls and crimson tablecloths. After sitting down and ordering a tomato juice for her and a lager for him, they perused the menu. She noted his fine hands, with long fingers and well tended nails. He had a gold signet ring on his left hand, and he smoked cigarettes from a blue packet with a dancing gypsy on the front, *Gitanes*.

"Do you smoke?" he asked politely.

"Not at all," she responded, trying not to show that she didn't like smoking either.

"What would you like to eat? A steak? I'm having one."

"Oh, no, thanks. I'm a vegetarian."

"A baked potato then, or a salad?"

"Well, I don't usually eat a lot at lunchtime." This was an understatement of course. Rose was not used to eating cooked food, given her financial circumstances and restricted diet of apples or carrots

"You must have something. I can't eat a steak while you have nothing."

"OK, then. I'll have apple pie."

"With cream?"

"No, thanks."

"Ice cream?"

"OK. That would be nice."

Clearly the young man thought this was unusual, but he

didn't make a fuss, just ordered the dessert as she wished. The conversation went well. They took up where they had left off in the street the previous week. Nabeel, a Palestinian, was very interesting to curious-minded Rose, whose primary school stories had included *Ali Baba and the Forty Thieves.*

"So, tell me about your time here in England. Were you a student?" she asked.

"Yes, I finished my Higher National Diploma (HND) in Marketing at the Polytech last summer. Now I'm trying to find a job. I've been here five years already."

"Did you study English?"

"Yes, because I found spoken English very difficult. At first my brothers placed me in a work situation in a factory in Blackheath. The Cockney accent was so strong, I couldn't understand a word anyone said to me. I told them to speak English!"

"I bet that went down like a lead balloon!"

"You mean?"

"Sorry, it's a metaphor. They didn't like you telling them that?"

"They laughed, but they couldn't speak differently, so I got my oldest brother to pay for language study, here in central London. Of course, that meant that I met only foreigners. It's nice speaking to English people for a change."

"I see. What kind of work are you looking for?"

"Well, any business position would be fine. I just want to get some experience before I go home to work with my family. They have a construction and trading company in Kuwait."

"But you are Palestinian, aren't you?"

"Yes, lucky enough to have a Lebanese passport,

which means I and my family can get visas and travel. The Lebanese Government gave nationality to Christian Palestinians who'd fled Palestine when Israel was created. Most Muslims are stuck in refugee camps still, only able to travel if they can get hold of a *laissez passer* document."

"Gosh. It's all very new to me. We didn't study anything in school about twentieth century history, so I know very little about what happened in the Middle East. I'm sorry."

"No need to apologise. Although many Palestinians hate the British Government for how they handled the Middle East, we know the people, especially the young like you, know nothing about it. It wasn't your fault."

The apple pie and steak arrived at this moment, helping them to change the subject. Rose was intrigued to hear Nabeel ask for a slice of lemon. When the generous wedge was brought to the table he squeezed its juice liberally over his steak, not the French fries!

"Excuse me for staring, but I've never seen anyone eat steak with lemon juice."

"I don't know why I like it. I just do. We eat a lot of dishes with lemon in them, perhaps that's why. Now what about you? How is your bar job? How are your studies going?"

"Well, I had to get a job because I went to the USA in summer and I borrowed money from my brother. Since I paid him back I'm living on a very small income. I'm studying French, Italian and Secretarial Studies. I didn't know what to do after finishing my French degree. So I thought it would be interesting to come to London and study for another year. I have to go to France for ten weeks in the second term, after Christmas. Then I'll decide if the secretarial/translating world is for me."

"I see. And your family?"

"Home is in the East Midlands, near Nottingham."

"Ah, Robin Hood Country!"

"That's right - though it's not as romantic as in the films. My world is that of coal mines. My father is a mechanic and my mother works, too, because they're divorced. And I have a younger brother and a sister as a result of their separation, but those two don't even know each other! What about your family?"

"Both my mother and father are dead. My mother died in childbirth in Haifa, Palestine, in our big house, divided into flats. My father didn't think there would be a problem with her sixth child. It was a girl, but my mother didn't survive. The baby lived for a week or so, suckled by a Jewish lady who rented one of our apartments and had a small baby."

"How awful. So how did your father cope after that?"

"Well, it was difficult because even though we had aunties and uncles my father was proud. He never remarried. He relied on my sister, who was around 12 at the time, to look after us all. She never finished school because of the tragedy, and she never married because although she was beautiful, she was very independent, and never found anyone good enough."

"I see. What about your other siblings?"

"Siblings?"

"Any other brothers and sisters?"

"Another sister, who married a cousin. She lives in Beirut with her six children."

"Wow. And brothers?"

"Four of them."

"So five boys and two girls. And only one is married?"

"Yes, our background has made us very choosy!" This was said with a broad smile.

By now, their meals were finished, and Rose refused coffee as she had to get back to her classes. She was intrigued by this young man's story. She had limited experience and knowledge about Jews, but she knew nothing of the Zionist takeover of Palestine. It was all fascinating. They agreed a date to meet again, for a home-cooked lunch at Rose's flat in Clapham. Rose was keen to get Marie's opinion of him before proceeding further.

"You can bring a friend if you like. My flatmate Marie will be joining us."

"OK. That will be fine. I have a Greek Cypriot friend who has a car so we can drive over."

"See you soon, then."

Rose thought it would be interesting to learn more about this unusual person but she was a little concerned about the upcoming lunch because she had not cooked anything in the flat before. Both girls ate toasted snacks at home, so this was a big event. She planned for her staple hostess dish: chicken curry with lentil dahl and rice. She had to rush the shopping and cooking on the Saturday morning, and was worried about being late for the visitors' arrival. However, they were late too, so that was no problem. She had bought some beer to accompany the meal and Theo and Nabeel arrived with two bottles of wine.

Marie played hostess with the glasses while Rose served the meal.

"I hope you like curry?" she asked, as they sat down.

Neither man replied, but Nabeel asked, looking at the bowls of food in front of him,

"Where's the bread?"

"The bread?" replied Rose in amazement. "There isn't any bread. This is an Indian meal. Indians eat naan or chapati or roti, but I haven't made any of those, I'm afraid. I thought you'd like rice."

"OK," said Nabeel, looking rather disdainfully at the food. The two men served themselves, Nabeel eating minimally, while Theo, a roly poly guy with long black hair, tucked into the food with gusto.

"It's good," he said, sighing with contentment. "You can cook," he asserted.

"Thanks," responded Rose. "Is the chicken OK with you, Nabeel?" she asked.

"Cocorico," he crowed, unexpectedly, flapping his arms like wings.

"What on earth do you mean?" she asked in amazement.

"I am a chicken," he replied without further explanation. A slight chill settled over the group as Rose felt offended at the offhand response to her hard work. Marie tried to keep conversation going.

"Do you smoke? I have some cheap cigarettes for sale. I get them from work."

Both men were smokers and jumped at the chance to buy some cheap ciggies.

"Can we have a cigarette now?" asked Nabeel.

"Yes, but we don't smoke, so would you mind going outside?" Marie asked.

"Actually, we have to leave now anyway, so we'll say goodbye and thank you," he retorted.

Rose looked at her watch. The lunch had lasted exactly 90 minutes.

"Fine, see you around," she responded, not expecting to see either of them again.

As Rose washed up while Marie went back to bed to rest up before her evening job, she wondered about the strange behaviour of her new 'friend'. She didn't care if she saw him again or not. But the following Monday lunchtime, there he was again in the canteen. He came up to Rose with a single red rose in his hand.

"Sorry about Saturday," he apologised. "Theo drives so badly I was feeling exhausted when we found your place. And I'm not too keen on chicken, either."

"Never mind," she replied. "It doesn't matter." But it did. She had been disappointed as well as offended by his rudeness, but she was willing to give him the benefit of the doubt.

"Would you both like to come over for a meal at my place next weekend? Theo will join us if you like."

Rose was pleased that visiting Nabeel's home with so little prior knowledge of him they would have the company of Theo.

"I'm not sure if Marie will be able to come, because she needs her sleep in the daytime."

"OK. I'll cook for three. See you around 2 pm, OK? That will give me time to make the food delicious."

That Saturday she dressed with care in her orange miniskirt and black twinset edged with psychedelic stripes of orange and green, and painted her nails a matching shade of orange. Then she took the Tube to Gloucester Road and walked the short distance to Nabeel's bedsitter. She found the house, rang the bell and Nabeel ran down to escort her upstairs to his top floor room. As they went upstairs she could see through an open door a bathroom, and another separate toilet. It all seemed rather down-market and seedy to her.

At the top of the house the trees outside the window made the view attractive.

"It's like living in a bird's nest," she exclaimed.

"Yes, it's nice and quiet up here. No one walks on my head," Nabeel told her.

Theo came in, laughing and joking as usual, and smoking too. They drank an aniseed, milky white drink called *arak* which she had never tasted before.

"It's a special drink from Lebanon. Very strong, be careful."

"I like strong drinks, don't worry," she assured him, sipping the strange new beverage in its small glass.

"It's good for your digestion," proclaimed Theo. "We drink it in Cyprus too."

"OK. It's good. I like it," Rose told them. "It's like Pernod, the French drink."

"I've made an Arabic dish for you. It's *kofta bi saniya*. Minced lamb with parsley and onions. With mashed potatoes. And salad."

"I'm sorry, I don't eat red meat," Rose told him. "But I can eat the sauce."

"Oh, good. It's sesame seed sauce. Very delicious, with lemon juice and garlic."

"Sesame? Like the spell in the children's story...Ali Baba and the Forty Thieves?"

"Sorry? What's a spell?"

"Let me think... There's a children's story ... I forget the details... but Open Sesame is what Ali Baba says to the door to the cave with all the jewels inside."

"Open Sesame? Ah yes, *Ifta ya Sim Sim*! That is Open Sesame in Arabic. It's a joke! Sesame seed is *sim sim* in Arabic. This dish has sesame seed oil in it."

"That's interesting! I've never had it before. It's very nutritious, isn't it?"

"I don't know about that. But it's delicious. That's what matters!"

Rose tasted a little before pouring some onto her mashed potatoes. It was indeed delicious, as was the salad dressed with lemon juice and olive oil.

As before Theo benefited the most from the meal, thanking his host before withdrawing to his room next door to study. Nabeel and Rose washed the dishes in the tiny kitchenette together and stored the leftovers in the tiny fridge.

"Would you like to go for a walk in Kensington Park?" he asked. "It's not far from here."

As they walked up Gloucester Road towards the Park in the mild autumn weather, the conversation, which had been stilted over the meal, began to flow. Rose had so many questions to ask, and Nabeel was not slow at explaining his past and the Palestinian tragedy to her. As they circled the Peter Pan statue they talked without noticing time passing.

"Come back and have a drink before you go home," Nabeel suggested as they got back to the Tube Station. It was a tempting offer, as she felt she had got to know him better after these few hours together and she felt huge sympathy for his background.

"OK. Why not?"

Back in the bedsitter they drank some red wine and talked some more. Once again time flew and suddenly Rose realised she should be taking the train to go home.

"I have to go," she said. "I don't like travelling on the train when it's dark."

"Why not have some supper and stay tonight?" asked Nabeel. "I'll uphold that principle you told me about."

She laughed. "Good. I've had it a long time and I'm not letting it go."

"I'll make you Welsh Rarebit," he said proudly. "With grilled tomatoes."

And indeed he did, using the grill in his kitchenette with flair, so that the cheese on toast was browned to perfection, with some fresh, tangy tomatoes and Worcestershire Sauce on top.

"Delicious. Thank you!" Rose was hungry and after eating, tired. The two went on talking and sipping wine until finally they fell asleep, not waking until morning.

"Goodness!" thought Rose on awakening. "It's Sunday and my Mum will be calling me. I have to go home. And I need a shower!"

"Here's a towel," offered Nabeel. "There's soap downstairs."

It seemed very strange to Rose to be going downstairs in this tall house to a bathroom shared with unknown people in other bedsitters. There was no proper shower so she crouched in the bath and washed, first washing the bar of soap she found on the washbasin. After drying herself she put her clothes on again, and started up the stairs. As she left the bathroom a door opposite opened and a long-haired blonde girl came out.

"Hello!" The girl spoke with a slight accent and a soft, melodious voice.

"Hi!" replied Rose.

The two smiled at each other without speaking further. Rose felt slightly ashamed as she hurried up the stairs.

"I saw a girl come out of the room near the bathroom," she told Nabeel.

"Was she blonde or dark?" he asked.

"Blonde. Pretty. Nice smile."

"That will be Noreen," he told her. She's Turkish. She works in radio."

"Really? That's interesting. How many nationalities live in this house?"

"Well, Johnny the housekeeper is Greek Cypriot and so is Theo. Number 13 is Irish, Number 10 is English, Number 9 is Iranian, Number 8 too, 7 is the bathroom, Number 6 is Turkish, Number 5 is French, Number 4 is Turkish, Numbers 1 and 2 are the housekeeper's and Number 3 I'm not sure - the tenant changed this weekend."

"Wow. Well, I'd better get back home - after being away for 24 hours Marie will be worried about me. And Mum usually rings on Sunday mornings."

"OK. But let's see each other during the week, shall we?"

"Maybe. What will you be doing during the week?"

"I'll be looking for a job as usual."

"OK. Come by the College on Wednesday afternoon.

I'm working Wednesday night and I'll be leaving from there at 5pm."

"OK. Will do."

Rose rushed to the Tube and so to her flat. Marie was in bed, but woke up briefly to say Mum had called.

"Oh dear, thanks, Marie. Did you say anything to her?"

"No. She asked where you were. I said I didn't know cos I hadn't seen you since yesterday."

"Oh my word. She'll be worried. We haven't got a phone at home so I can't call her."

"Never mind, she won't worry, surely. You're an adult."

"I know, but I've lived a quiet life till now! Are you working tonight?"

"No, it's Sunday. Night off."

"OK. Let's go and get a pizza later. Go back to sleep."

"OK. Talk later, lover girl."

"Stop it! We're just good friends. You know me and my principle."

Rose set to work to wash her clothes by hand and put them to drip in the bathroom. She got out her books and began studying. *Memoires d'Outre Tombe* had been easier than Pitman's Shorthand. At around 5pm Marie woke up and they went out to get a pizza to share. As they went downstairs there was a heavy knock at the door. A large blue outline could be seen through the glass front door, which they opened.

"Good afternoon."

"Hello," they chorused.

"Does Rose live here?"

"Yes, that's me," said Rose, in surprise.

"Well, your mother has been in touch with us."

"Really? Is she sick? We don't have a phone at home."

"No, she was worried about you. She asked us to check you are OK."

"Oh, my word. I'm so sorry. I simply stayed overnight with a friend. Nothing is wrong. I don't know how to get in touch with her."

"We'll contact the local Police Station and pass on the message. Glad you are OK."

"Well, I'm very sorry she bothered you. I'm 23 you know, not a baby, but she worries about me as I was very ill in France a while ago."

"I see. That's OK. But keep in touch with her in future, OK?"

"Yes, thanks for your help. I'm sorry to bother you."

Rose felt terrible about causing Mum more stress. Mum knew nothing of her new friendship with Nabeel, so it was not surprising that she had gone into overdrive, worrying about her daughter in the big 'smoke'. After buying their pizza and enjoying it at home, she wrote a letter to Mum and went out to the postbox to mail it. In the '70s hard mail was the norm! Computers and mobile phones were unknown. Marie laughed when Rose explained where she had spent the night, since her own job meant she was out every night. She told Rose about one of her escapades with clients to cheer her up. She had been invited with another hostess to go to Paris with a couple of clients. The girls wanted to see Paris but they did not want to sleep with the men, who had only booked one room for the four of them. So the girls had slept in the bathroom, locking the door so that the men could not come in.

"There's safety in numbers," she told Rose, giggling.

With her principle about not having sex before marriage still entrenched, Rose gave a wry smile. So far through school, university and her year in France she had managed to avoid any challenge, but she was beginning to wonder if the struggle was worth it. She seemed to have feelings for this interesting young man who had come into her life. Would she stick to her principle now, she wondered? After all, she was 23 and it was unwanted pregnancy she really wished to avoid, rather than sex. She knew there was a birth control clinic, the Marie Stopes Advisory Centre, on Tottenham Road, which gave the new contraceptive pill to any woman who asked for it. She thought about making an appointment soon.

The following week was hectic, with studies and the part-time pub job on Wednesday and Friday evenings. On Wednesday Nabeel turned up in the canteen at 5pm as she was having a snack before work. Over a cup of tea he suggested she come back to his place after her pub shift, rather than go all the way home to Clapham.

"That sounds like a good idea. It won't be such a long journey at night on my own. Thanks."

The UK decimal currency had just begun to be used, so working at the pub was both physically and mentally challenging. Rose found the time passed quickly, though she could not say she enjoyed it. But at the end of her shift, when the closing bell had been rung, the landlord offered the barmaids a choice of unsold sandwiches, rolls or pies. Rose was feeling hungry after four hours on her feet, so she gladly chose two cheese rolls before running out of the pub to catch the train. When she got to Nabeel's she showed him her prizes.

"Look, I've got supper for us."

"Wow," said Nabeel. "You're actually going to eat something. Great. You eat both of them. I like to sleep comfort."

"What?" gasped Rose. "What does that mean?"

"It's a joke," laughed Nabeel. "In Beirut there's an advert for mattresses: *Sleep Comfort.* So if we are going to sleep in the same single bed, I need you to be a bit less skinny. We are both bony, so we'll hurt each other."

"I see. I suppose you have a point. Ho ho - no pun intended!"

"Would you like a drink?"

"Yes, please. Anything will do."

"How about some whisky? With ice? Do you like whisky?"

"Yes, I do. With water, please. It's too cold for ice."

"It's nice that you like whisky. It's my favourite drink. Not many girls like it."

"Well, I started drinking young. When I was eight my Mum used to give me a tiny glass of sherry as a treat for babysitting my brother, who was six. I was a very responsible drinker!"

Nabeel laughed. They chatted about his day and Rose's bartending experience. Nabeel was having trouble finding someone to give him a job. His age and qualifications were greater than his experience. He needed to find someone who would give him a start.

"It's really depressing," he said. "I have to find somewhere soon because my family want me to go back to Kuwait and join them in the family business."

"What kind of business?" asked Rose.

"They have a contracting and trading company. Two

of my brothers work on the trading side, the third is a civil engineer, so he does building projects."

"What kind of things does he build?"

"Fire stations, police stations, private houses. Right now there's a big tender for eight new hospitals in Kuwait. It's a really big deal if we can get it. We would have all the contracts for supply, buying in all the fittings, such as sanitary ware, so it would be great for the trading side."

"So they could do with your expertise there really? And you could gain some experience with them?"

"Yes, but it's very narrow experience. I'd prefer to work here and stay close to you."

"That's a nice thing to say."

"Come closer and I'll show you what I mean," he hinted broadly.

"Now, let's get this straight," remonstrated Rose. "I don't want to change the rules of this game. You and I are getting to know each other. So let's stay friends for now."

"OK," Nabeel said somewhat reluctantly. "You're right. But I hope we're going to be closer friends soon."

"We'll see. Good night for now. Let's get some sleep."

The next day after her second shared bathroom experience in the bedsitter house, Rose went into College wearing the same clothes as the day before but no one noticed. She got back to Clapham and saw Marie briefly before she went off to her own work.

"So how are things going with your love life?" asked Marie. "I noted your absence again last night!"

"OK, but I think I'm going to have to get to the Marie Stopes Clinic before things escalate," laughed Rose.

"I see," Marie said with an understanding smile. "Well, make an appointment then! See you soon."

"Bye for now. Take care of yourself!"

Rose didn't really approve of Marie's work. She worried that one day the clients might not be as respectful or as respectable as they had been so far. But Rose had her own life to manage too. The next morning she rang the Clinic from College and went along for an appointment. There was no fuss, just some simple checks on weight, height, blood pressure, family history, then an explanation of the need to take the pills every day at the same time, and a warning about missing a day or having sickness and diarrhoea.

"You will not be safe to have sex for at least two weeks from starting the pill," the clinic nurse warned. "And you will not be protected against sexually transmitted diseases such as chlamydia, syphilis and gonorrhea unless your partner wears a condom. You must remember that."

These were the days prior to HIV/AIDS, when the names of STDs themselves conjured up horrific images of their effects. Sailors and sex workers had been those most frequently exposed to them till now, but the Flower Power, Free Love generation of the Sixties and then the Swinging Seventies had led to them becoming more common amongst young people. Rose flinched a little, and wondered if this little pill was going to be more of a threat than she had imagined. There was clearly more to fear than pregnancy when engaging in sex these days. But at least she felt she would be ready should she decide to break with her principle.

She went back to College thinking about when to start her first packet of pills. They were lodged in a neat little pink case, with the days of the week marked on each little slot.

She had not got a firm date to see Nabeel. Perhaps she should wait and see if he persisted in seeing her despite her reluctance to engage in sex. He had told her he had had a German girlfriend before, who had returned to her home in Germany. Rose did not know if he was still in touch with her, perhaps hoping to renew their relationship some day. She was certainly not going to take a chance on being a one night stand. If she agreed to moving to the next level in this relationship, she wanted it to be a steady one. Time would tell.

Meanwhile, she needed to work on improving her shorthand and typing speeds. Her best friend on the course, Kate sat with her on the back row of the typing class so that they could exchange gossip about their romantic lives. Kate was hanging out with a young medic, and had leaped to the next level very soon after meeting him. She was often late for class, and her eyes were usually dark circled.

"Too many late nights," Kate confessed. "It's very demanding, my love life," she explained. "I spend more nights at his place than mine. I just go home to catch up with some sleep. But he's worth it."

Rose realised that if she started to do the same her studies would suffer and she could not accept that. Already working at the pub was taking some of the energy she should be spending on her French and English shorthand. Also, the Polytechnic's Postgraduate Diploma in Translation and Secretarial Studies required the students to spend ten weeks of their second term on work experience in the country of their first language. Rose was studying French and Italian, so she had been placed in Paris, at a bank on the *Champs Elysees,* which was an exciting prospect. She had never been to Paris, so it would be fun sightseeing as well as getting a taste of working as a translator.

October was now edging towards November and exams were looming before the Christmas break. From mid-December to mid-January Rose intended to stay home with Mum, working at the Post Office delivering Christmas mail to make some money. Living so far from the College and the pub was expensive, though staying at Nabeel's after the pub reduced the number of train journeys, helping her get her finances back on track. Also, she was saving on food, eating the pub food leftovers. She needed to keep the pub job until the end of term and was wondering what to do about the fares from Clapham when Marie dropped a bombshell. She was going to the USA with a new boyfriend! She wanted to leave the flat as soon as possible, giving the requisite one month's notice on 1 November. This provided Rose with the impetus she needed to find somewhere else to live.

She decided to look in the area near Nabeel's place for convenient Tube travel to College and the pub. She scoured the ads in South Kensington, Gloucester Road, and Earls Court, or Kangaroo Valley, as it was known for its myriad Ozzie residents. She finally found and was interviewed for a flat-share with four other girls, in SW5. The lease-holder had her own room and was involved in a stormy relationship. The other three girls shared two large double bedrooms, and she would be the fourth. Her roommate was called Marie too, a happy coincidence! It seemed to be fate and Rose moved in at the end of November. Theo and Nabeel came to Clapham in Theo's car to help move her stuff. She didn't have much but it made the move easier, so she was grateful. Thus began a new way of life, with proximity to

Nabeel making their meetings more regular and increasingly more intense emotionally. Nevertheless, Rose stuck to her principle and did not start taking her little pink pills.

Rose and Nabeel spent the last months of 1970 getting to know each other better, discussing the politics of the Middle East and both of them trying to achieve their goals: Nabeel to find a job and Rose to achieve faster speeds in shorthand and typing and understanding of French and Italian business studies. They didn't spend much money as their budget was limited, but Nabeel had a large circle of friends after spending several years in London, first as an English language learner, then as a student on the HND Business Program at Rose's College. He was a confident entertainer in his small bedsitter, preparing meals for around a dozen people at a time. He introduced Rose to Margaret, the Irish girl who lived in Room 13, and to Fay, a beautiful English girl who had dated his brother Joseph for a while. Fay had even visited Joseph in Beirut! Rose wondered if she would go there one day, and equally, whether she would be discarded one day. She stuck firmly to her principle for that reason too.

Another friend was a Jewish girl called Edna, so Nabeel could say in the most heated of discussions about Sabras (Jews born in the new land of Israel) "Some of my best friends are Jews!" This was a challenging time for Palestinians. Black September was formed after the PFLP (Popular Front for the Liberation of Palestine) blew up three planes in Jordan after hijacking them. As a result Yasser Arafat was forced out of Jordan to Lebanon. Rose did not know how much this affected Nabeel but he had jokingly showed her a pair of pants on which he had painted a skull and crossbones and told her he was a member of Black September. She did not believe him. He had no other Palestinian friends, and as a Christian, was happy to have the freedom to travel that his Lebanese passport gave him.

Johnny was a frequent guest, as was Theo, and so Rose also became familiar with the politics of Cyprus, Greece and Turkey. All this while drinking wine from Cyprus which Johnny was able to buy at a discount from a Cypriot restaurant in Camden Town. Rose learned that this area of North London was the Cypriot 'ghetto' area of London, where some grandparents could not speak English. Occasionally they would venture there in Theo's 'ash tray', i.e. his car. He hated stopping at traffic lights, so his route to North London was often circuitous. Rose wondered if he had any brakes, he was so keen not to use them. The couple were enjoying their time together so it came as a shock when Nabeel suddenly informed Rose that he would have to leave and go to Beirut for Christmas as his brother Joseph was getting married.

"To Fay?" asked Rose.

"Of course not," snorted Nabeel. "To a nice Catholic girl from Lebanon. I have to be there to support him as we have no father. It's important to show we are a solid family. The girl's family might not agree for her to marry otherwise."

"I see. So how long will you be gone?"

"Well, probably the last two weeks of December, coming back after New Year, like you."

"OK. So we'll be back to normal in January. That's fine. Have you booked your ticket yet?"

"No, I'm waiting for them to send me some money.

They have to pay for the ticket. But I'll probably be leaving on the 15th."

"OK. Do you want me to do anything in your place while you're away?"

"Not really. Just keep an eye on it. I'll give you a key. I'll only pay Johnny for December as I'm a bit short of cash. The family have stopped giving me my allowance now that I'm qualified. They still want me to go back and work with them."

"I see. I didn't realise that. Do you think they'll want you to come back here?"

"I'm not sure, but I hope so. I'll make it happen whatever they think."

"You might have to take any old job just to support yourself. Perhaps working in a cafe? You can cook or wash dishes at least!"

They both laughed.

"Let's hope it won't come to that," said Nabeel.

And so their relationship was put on hold while Nabeel returned to Lebanon and Rose to the Midlands to see her Mum and start her fulltime Post Office Christmas mail delivery job for the two weeks before Christmas. It was a cold, physically demanding job for Rose. She had not yet reached the first year anniversary of her major operation and one month hospital stay in France for an abscessed appendix but she was in desperate need of money after repaying her brother. Even with the pub job in the first term of her studies, she had only just got by. She followed the example set by Mum: Grin and bear! Just get on with what life dishes out to you. But Rose had plans in mind too. While she could work, she would, and change her life for the better.

12

Christmas, then Work Experience

MUM'S BIRTHDAY ON New Year's Day was an event the family liked to celebrate together. This year Mum was 43, still young in years, but the crippling disease RA was taking its toll on her physically. Her children had never been able to hug her, she was so fragile, but she had to go on working to support them. She was an intelligent, practical person with a strong work ethic. She was also the sole parent of a small child. Looking back now Rose was old enough to appreciate life's slings and arrows, she realised how desperate Mum must have felt in those days, when none of her children was working. Bill was in his third and last year at university, Rose was in her fourth year of grant supported fulltime studies and John was only seven. Mum must have wondered if Rose would ever support herself independently, but she never complained.

Despite her small budget Mum always managed to buy a turkey for Christmas Day lunch, and a piece of pork for New Year's Day. Pork pie was their traditional Christmas morning breakfast while the turkey was roasting and the vegetable side dishes were being prepared. They had traditional mashed and roast potatoes, as well as brussels sprouts, bread pudding, and cranberry sauce. Mum liked to get the vegetables prepared and the turkey stuffed on Christmas Eve, though Bill and Rose tried to persuade her to leave some jobs for them to do on Christmas morning. In the past they had always gone to Midnight Mass so that they were free to prepare lunch the next morning but gradually they had discontinued church attendance. Mum still believed in God but could not walk to church or afford to take a taxi, while the older two children had reached the age of reason.

This Christmas was the year of the apocryphal story of the burning tree. The old, artificial Christmas tree was decorated with tinsel, candle holders and treasured ornaments, as well as a modern, red and white glass spire which fitted right on the top. Real wax candles were lit in the evening when the family would sit together and sing carols around the piano. This year, suddenly, the tree caught fire. The instant conflagration was terrifying but Bill, with a *sangfroid* which John and Rose still admired, seized the small chrome pedestal base with his left hand, and with his right hand he flung open the front door which opened directly onto the street. With a superhuman effort he threw the burning tree outside and luckily no one was passing on this cold wintry evening. Bill's fast thinking and action prevented a disaster.

The rest of the holiday passed without incident. Bill and Rose visited Dad, his wife and five-year-old daughter, their sister, to share the Christmas spirit and home-made mince pies. They also visited Dad's Mum. Gran was still living in the village, but now a widow, she was contemplating moving from the two-storey house to a retirement village.

Back in London in the New Year for the Spring Term, Rose and her peers were preparing for their work placements abroad. Rose was to work in the Head Office of a major bank in Paris. Another placement in Paris was given to Jacqueline, a tall girl with an upper-crust accent, who became friends with Rose as a result of the upcoming placement. She had a boyfriend, Daniel, who was living with his family while she was living with her sister in an outer London suburb. It was not easy for the two to get together. They discussed the possibility of a bedsitter vacancy so Rose spoke to Johnny about it. He was pleased to see her.

"Hi Rose, how are you? How's Nabeel?"

"I'm fine," she said, "but I'm not sure about Nabeel. I haven't heard anything from him so I don't know what's going on. I thought maybe the mail from Lebanon was a bit slow."

"I haven't heard either, and you know the rent is due on his room."

"Oh, my word! Of course. Well, he was sure about coming back, so I'd better pay up."

"Can you afford it?"

"Not really, but I guess I'll have to."

"Thanks. I can't afford to cover the rent to the owners. I'd have to let it out again. But you could get your friend to pay if she moved in, couldn't you?"

"That's a good idea. I'll talk to her."

When Rose broached the subject, Jacqueline was very pleased, except for the size of the rent.

"I can't afford more than five pounds a week," she said. "I'm very sorry."

"Well, look," suggested Rose. "It's all very uncertain anyway, but if you agree that should Nabeel return suddenly, you'll give up the place, then I'll pay the remainder. That will be better for me. I can't really afford 7.50 pounds every week. 2.50 will be easier. It will be a stretch for me but I don't want Nabeel to lose his room, assuming he still wants it."

And so Nabeel's place became Jacqueline's place. Rose packed up Nabeel's clothes and personal possessions in a suitcase but she kept his dressing gown on her own bedroom door in the shared flat. The kitchen utensils stayed, because Jacqueline would need them. However, the two girls were due to set off for Paris at the end of February for ten weeks. So a second sublet was set in place. Daniel decided to take over the room while Jacqueline was away. After that they would live together and take over the whole rent, which would be a financial relief for Rose as she would have no bar job while in France.

So Jacqueline's relationship was moving along nicely, while Rose's was stalled, though why, she had no idea. She realised Nabeel must have met with a problem from his family. She had a mailing address but no phone number for him. She wondered if he had given up on the relationship because she had not given up her principle. If so, then her attitude was "good riddance to bad rubbish". She was not going to be blackmailed into having sex before she was ready for it. Edna came over to see her, to find out what was happening. She warned Rose that he might not be coming back. With her broader knowledge of the Middle East, she spoke from experience. Rose took the warning calmly but it tested her loyalty and made her more determined to stand by him and wait for him. Deep down she felt he was being prevented from returning as he had warned her that his family wanted him home with them.

Meanwhile, she and Jacqueline were due to catch the train to Dover, then take the Hovercraft to Paris on Saturday, 6 March. Over the weekend they would have to find somewhere to live in Paris. On Friday at College they agreed to meet at 6am at the bedsitter to catch the Tube to Victoria, then the 7.30am train to Dover. Rose was keeping her place in the flat and paying her rent in advance there, so money was in short supply. She said goodbye to Marie and the other girls on Friday evening. At around 8pm the young woman in the complicated relationship set two places at the small kitchen table for herself and her loved one as usual for breakfast the next day. Rose marvelled at this domesticity. In her adrenalin-driven world there was no plan for breakfast, just a mad dash for a cup of instant black coffee then a rush to the Tube. However, this evening she got an early night so as to catch the train.

The morning was dry as Rose pulled her little wheeled trolley along the street to Jacqueline's. When she reached the steps of the house there was no sign of Jacqueline. She rang the bell and Jacqueline's head poked out of a window high above.

"I'm sick. I haven't slept a wink all night. Can you come up?"

"Oh, my goodness," said Rose, pushing the front door open and leaving her case in the hall. She ran up the stairs and surveyed the limp, pale-faced girl in front of her.

"Come on Jacqueline, we have to catch that train. Just clean your teeth, get dressed and then close your case. Daniel can bring some more stuff later if you haven't got enough."

"OK," Jacqueline said weakly as she changed her clothes.

"Got your handbag? Ticket? Passport?" Jacqueline nodded as Rose dragged the small case downstairs. "We'll get a cab. It will save time and I can't pull two cases as well as you!"

They got a taxi as soon as they walked onto Gloucester Road. So early on Saturday morning the roads were empty and the cab quickly made up for the time they had lost. Jacqueline explained she had gone out for dinner with Daniel and they had had shellfish. It must have been off. The girls crossed their fingers as the cabbie drove maniacally through the still empty streets. As the taxi pulled up to the train station at Victoria the clock showed 7.20am. They had just about made it. An official kindly pointed out the Dover train, which was standing with the guard at its end, holding his green flag. The girls staggered to a second class coach, then collapsed into a seat as the train pulled out.

"That was a near thing," gasped Rose. "I'll get you some water."

Jacqueline nodded and murmured her thanks. She was asleep for the rest of the journey to Dover and rather sick on the Channel crossing. Fortunately she began to recuperate on the train into Paris, so that by the time they were in the *Gare du Nord* she was able to pull her own small suitcase along to Rose's great relief.

"Right, first we need to find somewhere to stay - if only for tonight. Let's head for the Left Bank. It's the student area, and supposed to be quite cheap."

Neither of the two girls had stayed in Paris before but they knew how to manage the Metro. They had brought traveller's cheques with them so they changed some money before they left the railway station. They needed enough francs to get by over the weekend and to pay for at least a week's stay in advance. They emerged in *Denfert Rochereau* and began to enquire of the concierges in all the small hotels in the area. Eventually they received a good tip about a small place on *Boulevard Raspail*. It was now late afternoon and they were getting desperate. They were pleased to learn that there was a double room with shower and toilet *ensuite*, and the price was low enough for the two of them to afford. Both their work placements were on the *Champs Elysees* so they would be able to meet after work each day. Breathing a sigh of relief they unpacked, took showers and went off to find some food.

The area they were to live in was not particularly interesting, so they walked down to the more buzzing Left Bank. They looked at menus posted on cafe doors, and realised that neither *Table d'Hote* nor *A la Carte* dishes were within their budget. But along the streets there were *crepes* stalls and pizza vendors, so they bought thick slices of pizza with black olives and anchovies embedded in the tasty Gruyere and Emmenthal cheese topping.

"Shall we share a crepe for dessert?" asked Rose.

"Why not?" said Jacqueline, "I'm feeling so much better now!"

They watched as the young lady made their crepe, swirling the batter swiftly and evenly around the huge hot plate. Then she deftly spread sweet chestnut paste all over it and folded it into a tube.

"S'il vous plait, est-ce que vous pouvez la couper pour nous a partager?" asked Rose carefully.

"Bien sur." With one deft slice from her spatula she divided the crepe into two and wrapped one end of each piece in a small piece of paper. *"Voila,"* she said as she handed the sweet treat over to the girls. Munching on their pancake piece the girls found their way slowly back to the hotel, noticing the lights of couscous restaurants and kebab houses as they went.

"They could be cheaper places to eat in future," Rose suggested.

There would be lots to investigate the next day, Sunday, so they got themselves into bed for a much needed night's sleep. The next morning they could hear distant church bells when they woke. It was strangely pastoral despite the city context.

"I'm sure there'll be a Sunday market somewhere," Rose mused.

"Oh yes, that's highly likely. We can get some food really cheaply there - some cheese and bread and tomatoes for our lunch! We might even find somewhere to get some wine," Jacqueline replied enthusiastically.

"I'm not sure we should really start spending money on wine," Rose responded doubtfully. "Let's see how we cope with the budget for the food we need for existence first!"

"You're right - but we can look, can't we? *lecher les vitrines*, you know!"

"Of course. That will be fun."

The day was dry if not yet sunny as they made their way out of the hotel, calling *Bonjour* to Mme. la concierge as they left. After only one night they had settled into their new home for the next ten weeks.

"Wait a moment," called Rose to Jacqueline as she dashed back into the foyer.

"Madame, est-ce qu'il y a un marche ce matin pres d'ici?"

"Mais oui, Mademoiselle. Au coin. Ca finit a midi, vous avez encore deux heures."

Reaching the corner they could hear the cries of the market cheese sellers, fruit and vegetable vendors, and some stalls for *bric a brac*. Nearby the smell of freshly baked baguettes and roasting coffee was temptingly aromatic. The girls shopped for a simple picnic lunch. They walked on towards the Seine to find a pleasant spot to eat. They finally found themselves in the *Tuileries*. Happy family groups were strolling along the paths lined with spring flowers. It was idyllic sitting on a park bench, but then they realised they had no knife with which to cut the bread, cheese or tomatoes.

"Well, you know fingers were made before forks," laughed Rose as the two girls began breaking crusty pieces off the baguette and pulling the soft, white, fragrant Camembert apart. They nibbled the tomatoes carefully so as not to get covered in juice.

"Mmmmm, this is delicious, isn't it?" Jacqueline murmured.

"Indeed - *dejeuner en plein air,* to steal a title from a famous painting? Renoir? That reminds me, shall we make a day of it and go to the Louvre after this?"

"Sure. That's a great idea. I wonder how much it costs?"

"It might be free if we are lucky. Like the British Museuem! Fair exchange, after all."

Although they had to pay an entry fee, they spent several

hours wandering around, searching for painters they had heard of, especially the Impressionists and of course, the Mona Lisa. The small painting of the wistful lady was slightly disappointing but they had to agree it was charming, and her eyes did seem to follow them as they walked in front of it. In those days, Rose recalled, there were no crowds around it as today.

"My feet are aching," muttered Rose.

"Mine too," confessed Jacqueline. "Let's get out of here. Are you hungry?"

"Not really. We've got some lunch left."

"Shall we get a beer in a cafe and then go 'home' and finish our picnic?"

"Yes, let's. We've spent enough for one day."

On foot again, to save the Metro ticket, the girls wandered along the streets until they came upon a small cafe with pavement tables, where they ordered a beer - *pression* was the cheapest - which they drank thirstily before continuing back to the hotel.

"We need to get an early night again. We have to get the 8am Metro at the latest. We'd better not be late on our first day."

Rose set the alarm for 7am to allow them both to take a shower and walk to the station. Both girls had an appointment with the management in their different places of work on their first day. As yet they did not know exactly what their duties would be. It was exciting but slightly nerve-wracking to contemplate moving from being a student to being a professional, even if only for a *stage*. Saying good night to each other they drifted off to sleep, slightly concerned about the coming week, but happy with their achievements so far in finding somewhere to live within budget. Rose made a mental note to buy a post card for Mum at lunchtime the next day. She wanted to pass on the good news.

The spring weather in Paris was mild that year, though the mornings were chilly. For work on day one Rose chose her miniskirted brown tweed suit - made by Mum of course- with a pale pink sweater underneath it, pale pink tights and her clumpy, brown patent leather, Charles Jourdan shoes, bought from Marie. She felt quite the *Parisienne* as she glimpsed the reflection of her slim figure in the huge shop windows on the *Champs Elysees* on her way to work that first day. She was introduced to *Madame la Directrice* in the Translation and Foreign Transaction Section. After a few words of welcome Madame handed her over to the head of section, who explained the duties and introduced her to fellow workers. There were two other English girls, both married to Frenchmen, so not keen on striking up a close friendship with someone who would be on board for only ten weeks.

Her job on the first day would be the same for the first week, opening letters in three languages, English, Italian and French, date stamping them, and clipping them together then distributing them to the person they were addressed to. These persons were all male. Clearly they were superior to the task of opening their own letters, but they did not have their own personal secretary, so the department dogsbody, Rose, was to open them. She didn't mind at all. The task was easy and interesting as she had never worked in a bank. By Friday, however, she was looking forward to the next week, when she would have another task. And so it would go on over the ten week period until she was upgraded to the real task of translating incoming letters and finally taking dictation and typing outgoing letters. Faxes were not included as the fax machine required special skills and was rather temperamental.

Rose was pleased with her job and glad she was not in Jacqueline's position at the expensive car showroom. Her work there seemed rather slow and boring but had the opportunity to meet some big spenders, whereas Rose was always busy so the time passed quickly. In the mornings she usually had to rush to work because the system at the bank was for the workers to sign on in the morning. If they were late they were obliged to go to *Madame la Directrice's* office and explain their tardiness. Madame was a stickler for punctuality and Rose was infamous for her inability to be on time. She liked the adrenalin rush of cramming in tasks before she was due anywhere, so almost inevitably she was late for appointments. However, Madame's dour face was enough to sharpen up her habits. Rose enjoyed dressing for work, either in her light woollen suit, or in one of her two dresses, a warm turquoise jersey with long sleeves, the other a short sleeved style in a lighter black and white nylon material or in her terracotta jersey trouser suit. She had only one pair of shoes for work, but she allowed herself to purchase a pair of high, strappy, brown patent leather sandals and a pair of black leather clogs with high heels and wooden soles. With her mini skirts and new shoes, and her tinted lenses she felt confident and attractive for once in her new life.

After work Jacqueline and Rose met up and satisfied their hunger cheaply by ordering black coffee at the bar (no tip required) and taking several individually wrapped sugar cubes (two to a pack) which they ate while drinking the strong, bitter coffee. In this way they could get by with only one meal a day, in the evening, after doing some more sightseeing together. They managed to see a lot of Paris together, until on the fifth weekend Daniel came over to stay for a couple of weeks, so Jacqueline rented another room for the two of them. This meant Rose was at a loose end, but ever resourceful, she decided to take a long walk to revisit the *Tuileries* as they had done the first weekend. As she strolled along she felt at ease and happy with her lot. Taking this course and completing the *stage* had not been an easy undertaking but it had helped her commercial French and it had shown her that she could work in a bank if she needed to. Suddenly her thoughts were interrupted. She became aware of someone standing in front of her: a tall, slim, good-looking young man with fair hair and steel-rimmed glasses. He was smiling and had obviously just spoken to her in French, but her immediate memory only caught the last word, *mademoiselle*.

"*Plait-il?*" Rose uttered in a daze, wondering if this was the correct phrase for 'pardon', meaning "What did you say?"

"*Est-ce que vous avez l'heure, Mademoiselle?*" the young fellow repeated.

Looking at her white enameled metal, faux Chanel watch, Rose informed him in French that it was midday. He smiled again and asked her if she was English.

"*Mon accent me trahit?*" asked Rose with a laugh.

"*Mais non, vous parlez tres bien le francais, mais vous portez un plan de Paris en anglais!*"

"*Ah, je comprends!*" laughed Rose. "My map has given me away."

Although this was obviously a 'pick up', the young man was attractive, nicely dressed and his manner of speech was pleasant so Rose was quite agreeable to having her solitary walk interrupted. The two of them continued talking and walking, as he explained he was an engineer, from Lyons, just visiting his sister for the weekend. His name was Alex. He had no plans other than to enjoy himself, and Rose delighted in his company, thrilled to be speaking a mix of French and English. They spent the day together, found a small cafe for dinner that evening, and spontaneously spending the night cuddled together, though Rose still stuck to her no premarital sex principle. On Sunday morning Jacqueline and Daniel were somewhat amazed to meet Alex. Rose's risk-taking trait was clearly developing.

The four of them had lunch together and hearing of Daniel's plan to stay and spend Easter weekend with Jacqueline, Alex suggested that they might spend the long weekend in the South of France. He would meet their train in Lyons on Good Friday and drive them to Avignon, then return them to Lyons on Easter Monday to take the train back to Paris. Rose immediately got in touch with Brigitte, to ask if they could stay with her for the weekend. As luck would have it Brigitte and her family would be in Geneva visiting her parents. Nevertheless, she was willing for them to stay in Avignon at her new place. She left a key with her neighbour so they could get in. Rose was excited to spend the weekend with Alex and to revisit Provence where she had spent such an eventful year. Amazing good fortune!

Brigitte's new flat was beautiful. In the dining room there was a huge olive wood table with a massive olive wood bowl filled with walnuts gathered from local trees. The four made inroads into the pile that night, drinking liberally from the *cave*. Rose planned to restock it with suitable wines before they left. The next day they visited some of the wonderful places Rose had visited during her year as an assistant English teacher. They also went to some new places. The longest trip they made was to the fantastic Pont du Gard. The four were recklessly happy, and enjoyed their absent hosts' hospitality. Rose could not now recall, but she hoped she had left a suitably generous present for Brigitte. Their weekend was soon over, and the foursome headed back to Lyons and the trio thence to Paris.

Rose felt sad saying goodbye to Alex. She had quite forgotten about Nabeel while she was with her new friend, but now she wondered what the future held for them. Alex seemed smitten by her, and the two promised to write. In fact, communication was intermittent because they were both busy, but Alex expressed the hope that he could visit Rose in the UK. Rose, somewhat guiltily, agreed that he should, but explained that she would have to see how her course went before she could make a firm plan for a visit. Deciding as always that honesty was the best policy, Rose felt she needed to let Nabeel know that she was on the verge of a new relationship, so she wrote a long letter the following week, explaining what had happened, and saying that Alex was going to visit the UK. She therefore warned him not to come back before the visit was over, if he was, indeed, planning to come back. She reminded him that she had been paying his rent and had heard nothing from him. Conscience clear, she went ahead with plans for Alex to come over to London and meet her family. Ever since those early days when she had been ashamed of her working-class origins and her mining village home, she had not felt she needed to apologise for her background.

The two girls had to complete their *stage* and then return to complete their studies and final exams. An accolade from the *stage* was to be offered a permanent job. Much to Rose's amazement, in her final week at the Bank, she was called into the Personnel Office for an interview. There she was offered a place in the Department when she had finished her studies. She was *bouleversee* in French and gobsmacked in English. She really didn't know how to explain that although the work had been fine for ten weeks, there was no way she could accept a permanent position in such a dreary, monotonous job. She could not envision a career in secretarial work as her future. While she was searching for words, the Personnel Director helped her out:

"Je comprends, Mademoiselle. Vous avez un petit ami a Londres, peut-etre?"

Rose jumped at the excuse offered her. It was much more diplomatic than the truth.

"Mais oui, Monsieur, c'est ca. Je ne peux pas accepter mais c'est tres gentil."

They shook hands and Rose escaped back to the Department, breathing a deep sigh of relief. How on earth did they think she could work there? Even though Alex had now entered her life, a career in banking in Paris was not on the cards for her. She laughed once the shock had receded. It was a great compliment after all. She wondered if Jacqueline had had the same experience? After work they met as usual in the cafe between Place de la Concorde and Arc de Triomphe. They had both been complimented in the same way, but neither of them was willing to return. Rose hoped that this would not mean a *stagiare* would not be accepted in future. They had enjoyed their time in Paris and the work had not been arduous. Being an assistant to three men was not Rose's idea of work, she now fully realised.

At the last minute the girls picked up some souvenirs, including two kilos of freshly ground coffee. On their last night Rose could hardly sleep for the caffeine-laden air she was breathing! With some relief they got up on Saturday morning and made their way by Metro, now so familiar to them, to the *Gare du Nord* for their train and hovercraft trip home. There was no one to meet Rose at Victoria Station, but Daniel was there for Jacqueline. They took the Underground to Gloucester Road, where the happy couple returned to Nabeel's bedsitter, while Rose walked on to the flat to resume her student life. The *stage* had been an interesting interlude, with an added souvenir, Alex, but now the rest of the course lay ahead with final exams to take. Rose needed to wrap her head around shorthand and typing, rather than possible boyfriends, though both Nabeel and Alex kept crossing her mind.

Rose had not given a mailing address in Paris when she wrote to Nabeel, and when she checked her mail at home there had been no reply from the Middle East. Checking with Jacqueline the next day there had been no news at the bedsit either. So the status quo was resumed for the time being and studies came first. There was mail from Alex, however. He seemed keen to come over and resume their friendship. Rose made plans for him to stay in the flat with her, as her roommate Marie had a boyfriend with whom she could stay. They would do the sights of London during the week, go to Mum's for the weekend, then return to London for Alex' farewell. Rose was looking forward to seeing her French friend again.

Just before Alex arrived, a letter stamped in Kuwait, not Beirut, dropped into the letterbox. It was from Nabeel. He alleged that he had been kidnapped by his family, made to travel with them to Kuwait after Joseph's wedding, and then his passport had been taken from him, so that he had been unable to leave. Since he had no income other than what the brothers gave him, even if he'd had his passport he couldn't have bought an airline ticket to London. Rose gasped in amazement at the saga. At the end of the letter Nabeel promised he was doing his best to return. He thanked her for looking after the flat and promised to repay her. Obviously the information about Alex had had a galvanising effect. But things were still up in the air, and Rose had a visitor on the horizon. She also needed to alert Jacqueline and Daniel to the possible return of Nabeel, even though the date was still unknown. How complicated things suddenly seemed to be.

Meanwhile, plans for Alex's visit had to go ahead, and although there were doubts and worries in her mind, Rose was interested to see how she would respond to him on her own turf. Had their short friendship been a holiday romance? Alex arrived at Victoria Station the weekend the course finished in June. As well as visiting home, where Mum took kindly to him, and London, where the flatmates were impressed by his boyish good looks, the two made a short visit to Ipswich to see Caroline, her old school friend who was now married. Caroline was settled into the working housewife mode, with a lovely home and an apparently doting husband. Caroline expressed her approval of Alex, which continued the emotional struggle Rose was experiencing.

Although she had not moved to the commitment level with either man, she could not string both along. At some point she would need to choose.

Rose admired Alex' apparent maturity. Compared with the fun-loving, capricious Nabeel, Alex seemed more like herself, a serious person. Moreover, Nabeel's childlike financial dependence on his brothers worried her. But before Alex returned to France, Rose felt compelled to admit to him that she was not as free as a bird. The saga involving Nabeel was extremely complicated and Alex was not impressed by it. He was clearly hurt and on leaving indicated that he had put their relationship on hold. There was no point in doing anything else, she supposed. There wasn't going to be a duel at dawn. If Rose was going to give Nabeel another chance, then she was indeed saying goodbye to Alex.

"Bien, voyons ce qui va se passer. Au revoir."

Rose felt tears well in her eyes as she said goodbye at Victoria Station. Alex' friendship was much less complicated and could have been the perfect relationship for her. Why did she feel she had to give Nabeel another chance? Was it the sympathy she felt at his sad past, given the family and political situation he had grown up in? Did she feel he needed her more than Alex did? Why was she feeling this loyalty? Was it the financial commitment she had made?

Rose had no time to spend on reflection and recrimination as she was now searching for a job. Despite her new qualification, she had decided not to take up secretarial work. Instead she responded to an advertisement for summer school teachers at an English language school in Crystal Palace. The University Careers Office had offered her three choices: Teaching was the second. Rose crossed her fingers as she took the train to her interview. Adam was the charming, handsome principal and owner of the school, while Mrs Thyme was the friendly, capable woman who ran the school's administration. The initial contract was for July and August, with an option to continue into the academic year if both parties were satisfied. Rose was to start with elementary students so that her lack of experience would not show. As a successful language learner herself she was aware that she could teach English if she set her mind to it, but at that period of TESOL (Teaching English to Speakers of Other Languages) history, not many textbooks were available for teachers or learners of English as a second language. She was given a textbook with a supporting teacher's book: *Practice and Progress* for elementary students. She also searched the shelves in one of her favourite places, Foyles Bookshop on Charing Cross Road and found a title that she thought would help: *Teaching English to Adults.* The Italian Coffee Shop just opposite Foyles' side entrance was as much of an attraction as the bookshop: It was a handy place to get a cappuccino in those days.

Having chosen the teaching profession, it was a lovely surprise to be visited by her friend, Brigitte from Avignon. She was accompanying a school group on a visit to the UK. As Rose did not drive they took a coach to meet Mum and see a little of Robin Hood Country. Brigitte was having some marital problems, which made Rose believe that she was right not to contemplate marriage in future. After hitching a ride from the Midlands down the M1 to London in a Jaguar they had fun visiting landmarks like Trafalgar Square, Carnaby Street and Buckingham Palace.

Rose's preparation time for the new classes in July

was punctuated by the sudden return of Nabeel in time to celebrate his birthday at the end of June. He brought her a gold bejewelled ring from Beirut and two mother of pearl necklaces as well as some cedar wood souvenirs for Mum. The presents were attractive but they did not make up for the long absence without communication. The stress and the expenditure on Nabeel's rent that Rose could ill afford required some convincing explanation. It was also intriguing to Rose that as soon as she had written about Alex, Nabeel had managed to break out of his 'imprisonment'. There was another issue on her mind, though.

She had been faithful to her principle ever since Nabeel left, but at the age of 23 she felt her virgin days should be over. She had almost given in to Alex, but he had not made any preparations for safe sex, so she had felt justified in sticking to the limits she imposed. With Nabeel back, showing he had missed her, she felt safe enough to commit to a complete sexual relationship with him and began taking the pills in the small pink container. Nevertheless things progressed slowly, Nabeel even questioning whether Rose was frigid, one sexual topic amongst many others, such as 'how to please your man' discussed in magazines like Cosmopolitan and Playboy at that time. He could not understand that she would not leap into bed with him.

"Did you have a problem before? Something in your childhood?" he had asked her.

"Of course not," replied Rose. But in fact, there had been issues in her youth which her conscious mind had blocked and which she only understood much later in life. She attributed her lack of arousal to the restrictions she imposed on her body all these years. With her platonic boyfriends she had been ashamed of the physical effects of sexual arousal and had repressed them. It did not strike her that perhaps this relationship did not have the right chemistry for sex. Instead, she blamed herself for the lack of spark and succumbed to repeated attempts to arouse here, including watching soft porn movies. But sex was not the only thing on Rose's mind after Nabeel's return to London. As usual, finance was an issue.

13

English Language School

THE STORY NABEEL told Rose about his months in Beirut and Kuwait and his escape from the family was dramatic but it also meant that he had no income, no money at all to live on. Jacqueline was willing to leave his bedsitter as promised. She had found a summer job on the South Coast as an English language teacher so moved out with Daniel. Rose decided to give up her shared room in the girls' flat and move in with Nabeel to save on his rent which she now paid as he had no family support. To help with costs, Nabeel was obliged to apply for jobs which would bring in some money, such as the despised dishwashing, while still searching for a job which would allow him to apply for a work permit. Meanwhile, he was on a visitor's visa after his previous six years' residence as a student. He was not forthcoming on the details and Rose was ignorant of these issues. All she knew was that she was happy, though concerned. Her life plan, such as it was, had not involved taking on someone who needed support. She had intended to be independent, but now she had become a provider!

For years afterwards Nabeel would joke: "I lived as a

bachelor in London for six years, but when I applied for a job washing dishes, they told me I didn't have enough experience." As with many of Nabeel's sayings, Rose could hear him laughing and lighting another cigarette after telling the joke. In fact, visa luck came his way courtesy of a Jewish man who ran a small printing company. Perhaps this small-business owner thought Nabeel too was a Jew, with his Semitic features and unusual name, or felt sorry for him as a Palestinian-born Arab. In exchange for a negligible salary, the owner processed Nabeel's work permit. This allowed him to search for more lucrative and more suitable positions. After about six months, when Rose's patience with the difficult financial situation was beginning to fray, Nabeel finally obtained a well paid marketing position with a French steel company based in St James Park. Finally, he could pay for his own bedsitter and Rose took on Number 13, a smaller, cheaper, neighbouring room which had been vacated by the sweet Irish girl, Margaret. Here she could spread out her textbooks and clothes, so as to study and get ready for work.

Previously, while Rose was sharing the flat she had met an Australian girl, a qualified teacher, who worked evenings in a school in North London. Falling suddenly ill and knowing Rose's educational background she asked if Rose would mind filling in for a few nights. Rose was extremely interested on account of the income as well as the potential career opportunity. She went along on the Number 73 bus from King's Cross armed with worksheets and ideas to handle a class of immigrants who needed language practice and English citizens who could not read or write fluently. Research in 1970 had revealed a million adults in London who were illiterate or semi-literate. A literacy campaign was launched to solve the problem, and Rose became involved in this. She enjoyed her teaching sessions so much that she applied to become a regular teacher and was accepted to teach two classes on two evenings a week in Stoke Newington for the Adult Education Institute (AEI).

At this point both Nabeel and Rose became very busy with work. Rose had a longish train journey to and from Crystal Palace five mornings a week. Two nights a week, instead of taking the train home she would take the Number 137 bus from Crystal Palace to Kings Cross and from there the Number 73 to Stoke Newington. Evening classes were held in a large day-school building where chalkboards were still in use. On these long journeys Rose ate sandwiches and read books on teaching English to adults. Given her longer work days and journeys, Nabeel was supportive, even making a cardboard clock with movable hands for Rose to use when teaching telling the time. He also constructed a flannel board with cardboard figures which stuck onto it with little velcro patches, as recommended in the teaching texts of the time. On Sundays the day school had excursions for the students to places of interest, such as Oxford, Cambridge, or Stonehenge. Class teachers were paid extra to lead the bus tours. Rose enjoyed looking up information to pass on to the students using the bus microphone. Sometimes Nabeel came with her, which made the excursions more fun.

There were also school parties, one especially memorable for the group of male Libyan students who were in London at the time. They were very lively so Rose asked Nabeel to teach her some words of Arabic which would get their attention and hopefully calm them down at times of extreme excitement. *Sulli an nabi* was the expression he taught her. To this day Rose was not completely sure of the translation but it had the desired effect of first, causing shocked silence, then laughter, and finally attention to the lesson in hand. One student, Mohammed Abyad, or Mike White, as the English translation of his name went, became a friend of the couple, visiting them in Central London, bearing gifts of Cleopatra menthol cigarettes. There was a lot to learn, but these friendships made life happier for Rose.

At school Rose progressed steadily through the curriculum, moving from Elementary to Beginners, with *First Things First,* the L.J. Alexander text which had line drawings to assist the learning process. Rose even now could recall the first lesson's dialogue:

Excuse me! Yes? Is this your handbag? Pardon? Is this your handbag? Yes, it is. Thank you very much.

Nabeel too was making progress. From experiencing extreme trepidation when handling phone calls to business people with regional accents, he began to make business trips to the foundry in North East France. He was proud to let his family know that he was making his own way and no longer needed their financial support. He did however retain one benefit from his older brother Joseph: his Playboy membership card. The Playboy Club on Park Lane was their preferred evening venue for dinner and dancing. As a member, the food was extremely cheap - just five sterling pounds for a steak, fries and salad dinner. Rose, of course, still a vegetarian, would have a baked potato and salad. They enjoyed disco dancing and could take a night bus home, so their outings were possible even on their small budget. They also went to the cinema or theatre most weekends, or concerts at the Royal Albert Hall and there were often dinner parties or larger social gatherings. Social as well as working life was busy.

But Nabeel and Rose's life together was not always calm. Both of them had strong personalities and Rose was jealous of Nabeel spending so much time with his many friends, both male and female. Often after Rose's long day at work someone would be at home with Nabeel waiting for her arrival either to go out to eat or for her to cook and eat at home. One friend, Fay, turned up from time to time, causing Rose to ask Nabeel if there was something between the two, or whether it was just a way for her to reach out to her former boyfriend, Joseph. Fay seemed a sweet girl, working as a hostess at sales events such as the Boat Show at the Earls Court Exhibition Centre. But the mail brought the biggest surprise one morning: a postcard from Heidi. This angered Rose as she read it and discovered that Nabeel had stopped over in Germany on his way back to London after his 'escape'. She was so distraught she packed a bag and went to Victoria Coach Station where she burst into tears while waiting for a coach home. Rose realised she would make Mum very unhappy if she turned up out of the blue, so with some misgivings she made her way back to Nabeel's where he did his best to allay her fears. But Rose wondered how much she could trust him after that bombshell. She disliked secrets, and she had been open about Alex.

Easter was punctuated by a visit from Joseph, tall, dark and handsome in an Omar Sharif way and far more charming in his manner and speech than his younger brother. They went to the Playboy with a young woman living in Number 6. A new resident, Claudine, was French, pretty, with long blonde hair and a strong, southern French accent. She was love-struck when she met the playboy Joseph, who continued to woo her while Nabeel and Rose went home to spend the long weekend with Mum. When Rose and Nabeel got back, the other pair had left for a romantic holiday in Europe which quickly concluded in marriage. No one was more surprised than Rose and Nabeel at this outcome but Joseph must have put in a good word for them with the family in Kuwait who were still smarting from Nabeel's 'escape'. They finally recognised that he was gaining international experience with his French employer so other members of the family occasionally made a 'reconciliation' trip to London.

Rose had already met Adel, Nabeel's younger brother, in the first phase of their relationship, and after Easter, Asma, his older sister and Edouard, one of his older brothers, came out to stay. Edouard registered Asma in a nearby language school, where she studied for a couple of months and stayed in Room 10. Rose began sleeping in her own room so as to keep up the modesty which Catholic Asma expected. The trio lived fairly happily together with both Nabeel and Asma sharing the cooking. Henri, the oldest and most difficult member of the family also paid a visit to the bedsitter some time later and insisted on Rose cooking him a curry, which he immediately said was not worthy of the name. Rose, who had learned homestyle North Indian cooking from her former boyfriend, paid no attention to his criticism.

"It's not a restaurant curry, it's an authentic, home-made curry. They won't taste the same," she told him. "And there are different styles of curry from different areas, so you can't expect them to be the same."

Rose resolved not to bother doing any more cooking for this revered older brother, but Nabeel seemed keen for her to look after him while he was at work. The memory was shameful to Rose now, but she recalled that after visiting the tourist sites on foot Henri had insisted they visit a cinema on Charing Cross Road, a place she had never been to, so that he could have a 'rest'. The movie was salacious if not actually pornographic, and Henri tried to force his aroused self into Rose's hand, when she thought he was offering her popcorn. In shock she stood up and walked out, waiting only a few moments in the foyer to see if he followed her. When he did not she went back to her bedsit and told the whole story to Nabeel later. After failing to support her when Henri criticised her curry, she wondered how Nabeel would react to this latest move. She was satisfied when he made sure that she did not see Henri again. He warned her that some Arabs believed that all English girls were 'easy'. He was very sorry that he had put her at risk with his brother. He had not expected this outrageous behaviour, he assured her but Rose wondered how naive he really was. Doubts stayed in her mind about this incident for a very long time.

The story behind the two oldest boys, Henri and Joseph was one of bitter rivalry. According to Nabeel Henri had faked his age at 14, saying he was 16 so that he could leave the refugee camp in Beirut and travel to the newly struck oil and construction camps in Saudi Arabia to earn a living. Instead of sending money home to his father and younger siblings he had gambled and spent money on women whenever he got the chance. Joseph on the other hand had joined a major Arab construction and trading company in Kuwait, and had learned the business from the bottom up. He had saved his earnings and looked after his brothers and sisters. In fact, the company run by Henri and Edouard now in Kuwait, was founded with his money, while he had kept himself out of the way for fear of conflict with his older brother.

Nabeel had benefited from the family company by being educated in England, while Adel had been allowed to complete his engineering degree at the American University of Beirut (AUB). Both of these youngest boys had done well in their different spheres, though Nabeel was the weaker in confidence and attitude. Nervous and uncertain of himself, he said he felt happy now he was apart from the brothers, but nevertheless Rose suspected that he would be going back to them sooner or later, to pay them back or to make his own fortune. She was not sure of his motives, but she did not have time to worry about them, since her life was very busy, working in two locations while still learning about TESOL. With her steady income she was now able to help Mum financially, so she was pleased. But she missed some cues which should have given her pause for thought.

First of all, the politics of the Middle East came to Europe, with the Munich Olympics Palestinian attack on the Israeli team in September 1972. Nabeel said nothing about this major incident as far as Rose could recall but she noted that he was sometimes quiet without explaining why. He was never happy when she needed to sleep after her long days at work and preferred to stay in her own room rather than with him at night. He once retaliated harshly in one of their frequent quarrels. "You're not good enough for me," he shouted.

In amazement Rose retorted "You need a dumb blonde,

someone who will put up with your addiction to TV wrestling and salacious stories in the *News of the World*."

Nabeel travelled a lot to Europe for his job, and he sometimes met up with family members there which seemed innocent enough. After all, Rose visited her Mum as often as she could. Family was important to both of them. But Britain had played an important part in the creation of Israel and the Palestinians were reduced to the status of a 'problem'. A British girlfriend might not be welcome on any other footing than a casual girlfriend. But she began to wonder if there was still contact with Heidi in Germany and jealousy crept into her mind.

14

Teacher Training

HAVING COMPLETED A year at the language school, Rose realised that she enjoyed teaching English, and needed to gain a qualification in the field. Garnett College had the only government-funded TESOL training course, but her application had gone in late and she was informed the course was full. So, keen to get into a course for the current academic year she applied to a North London college affiliated with London University, for a Postgraduate Certificate in Education (PGCE), with French as the major and English as a first language as the subsidiary subject. Having been accepted she was then surprised to receive a letter from Garnett saying they now had a vacancy. This was one of those pivotal moments in life when choosing, as Nabeel always said, was sacrificing. The decision was hard, because Rose had been brought up to stick to her word. She wanted to take the more focussed course in TESOL, but she did not want to go back on her acceptance of the alternative program. After some hard thinking about the additional opportunities which a secondary school French/ English qualification would give her, she turned down the

Garnett College offer and completed work at the language school in September.

From October every weekday morning Rose would travel to Tottenham to her College for her fulltime one year teaching course. It was government-funded as there was a need for teachers, so once again, Rose was lucky. There were two teaching practice phases in the education program: one in the second and one in the third term. The first was at a modern school in Walthamstow, which was fairly easy to get to. The French teacher Rose was partnered with reminded her of Brigitte, with her long, bleached blonde hair. The work was not arduous because the students opted for French. In schools where the subject was compulsory Rose's colleagues had a much harder time. In her second practice school in Barking she had both French classes as well as English classes with eleven year olds. The first year English students were intriguing in their naivete and expressed fondness for her. The students of French were far more enthusiastic than the Walthamstow teens had been. One even shouted out 'Mum' while raising his hand energetically, keen to be asked to speak!

Two afternoons a week Rose would walk down Tottenham High Street to her evening classes in Stoke Newington. She got on well with students and administration staff. At 9.30pm she would take the bus back into central London. They were long days, but invaluable for her Curriculum Vitae. She found the college lecturer in English particularly interesting, and never forgot his work ethic: "When you are really busy, then you are really living, so don't complain! Don't waste your life." From then on Rose made it her personal goal to achieve something new each year despite the continued hard work and long hours of study. The lecturers in French were more prosaic in their approach to teaching and judgemental in their assessments, which triggered Rose's lifelong interest in performance assessment.

She obtained her PGCE in June, having completed her written thesis on Comparative Education, though writing her thesis plunged Rose into a phase of compulsive eating. At University in her final year she had become anorexic, then bulimic and she was in danger of regressing under stress. Challenged by the writing task she ate slice after slice of bread to keep herself going. On those first nights spent together nearly three years previously Nabeel had thought she was saying her prayers, when she was counting her calorie intake for the day. Their relationship had saved her from anorexia because being with someone else encouraged her to eat proper food. But she was very concerned about gaining weight, looking ugly and having to buy larger clothes which she could not afford. Seeing how stressed she was, Nabeel reminded her of the menthol cigarettes Mike White had brought as a gift. Rose learned to smoke them in her own way, puffing out rather than breathing in. She still believed smoking was a dirty habit which made her mouth taste foul. But she smoked in her way, even trying brightly coloured Balkan Sobranies, until the thesis was completed and she could give up!

Rose's part-time position for the academic year had been fun and she had made a good impression on the Principal. With her degree, twelve months' TESOL experience and now a teaching qualification under her belt she felt ready to move into a career position in teaching. So when a fulltime position was advertised for Lecturer 1 in English, with the duties including Head of Department, Rose applied and was interviewed at County Hall, with a charming inspector who had earlier visited her classes, as the chairperson. She handled the interview questions as best she could, with the chairperson posing questions about details in teaching pronunciation, to which Rose responded with ideas such as using minimal pairs. At the end of the interview Rose was stunned when she was asked if she felt she could train other people to teach English. Of course she was obliged to say she could, but she wondered what lay behind the question as training others had not been on the list of qualities preferred or required. It was a compliment but it added another level of stress and on the other hand, another possible achievement to her future workload.

When she was informed a week or so later that she had been successful and was awarded the position, she was also asked if she could teach a class once a week in the evening at the central London AEI to prospective and current teachers of English! She had said she could, so she would, of course. Fortunately the classes would not start until after summer as she had an exciting holiday plan in place. There would be time after her holiday to plan for the first TESOL teacher training course she was to deliver. It would be the first of many more over a fifty-year teaching career, Rose reflected now. She had been a risk-taker in her field, but she had learned a lot from her practical experience, her reading of all the available texts, and her year in France as an assistant language teacher. At the time she had been as well prepared as anyone in her field and looking back with her doctoral degree completed, she knew she'd always done her best with students and teachers. She was satisfied in that area of her life.

15

Holiday in Beirut

THREE YEARS AFTER their first fateful meeting, Nabeel took Rose to Beirut. She excitedly planned her holiday wardrobe, making herself a trendy, halter-neck, maxi dress. The beautiful fabric printed with hibiscus flowers was as exotic as her holiday promised to be. She had bought the material in a sale at Harrods, an expensive store she visited occasionally to purchase Erno Laszlo's skin care products, found exclusively at Harrods. Marie, her air hostess friend, had recommended the regime for Rose's skin problems. She hated wearing makeup to cover pimples, so a healthy skin care routine was essential to her peace of mind. The products were expensive but the black soap eased the breakouts she suffered from. These problems with her skin contributed to her continued negativity about her appearance, including her eyesight and her weight. Nabeel did his best to shake her obsession with her weight, sometimes jokingly putting one foot on the scales behind her to shock her and make her laugh. Of course, the horror of the figure on the scales did not make Rose laugh. But she smiled when Nabeel generously paid for her to get contact lenses as her birthday gift that year. Casting off glasses in the daytime was a blessing she was grateful for and she still wore hard glass lenses, dinosaurs compared to modern, soft, disposable lenses.

Their flight to Beirut, dubbed the Paris of the Middle East in the '60s, was on Middle East Airlines (MEA) bearing the impressive symbol of the Cedars of Lebanon. Nabeel had written a thesis on tourism in Lebanon as part of his HND program in London. He was proud of his adopted country and obviously looking forward to showing Rose some of it in her brief visit. They went straight from the airport to his sister's apartment in the east of Beirut, the Christian district of Ashrafiya. As they travelled by taxi past a shambles of corrugated iron and cardboard shelters, Rose asked what the shanty town was.

"They are Palestinian refugee camps, Sabra and Shatila on the left and Burj al Burajni on the other side of the road."

"Palestinians are still in refugee camps here? But Israel was created in 1948, wasn't it?"

"Yes, and people fled here during the years before that, with the fighting and terrorism caused by Irgun and the lovely Messieurs Yitzhak Shamir and Ben Gurion, no longer terrorists, but proud members of the Israeli Government."

Rose was in shock. The quality of life afforded by these tumble-down shacks must be terrible. How could people improve their situation when they lived like this?

"How do they manage to live? How do they work and educate their children?"

"Well, Yasser Arafat is good. The PLO (Palestinian Liberation Organisation) has a social welfare program which gives families an allowance. The money comes from the wealthy Arab Gulf States, and also from those Palestinians like my family who are Christian and have managed to escape the camps. As I told you, we got Lebanese citizenship so we could travel with our passports. These people have only 'laissez passer' documents, which are not accepted by many countries. But within the camps those who are educated have set up schools to teach the young. Of course, some Palestinians migrated to Jordan and other Arab countries, such as Egypt where they have been able to work and travel. They support the PLO financially too."

"Thank goodness. I had no idea people were still unable to move on with their lives in this way."

"That's nothing. There is no right of return for these people, nor for us, while the Israelis humiliate those Palestinians who have been strong and stubborn enough to stay in our land. They punish any protests severely, usually imprisoning the perpetrator of the protest, but also by destroying the house of his or her family. The suffering experienced in the Holocaust taught some Israelis oppression and brutality, rather than sensitivity and understanding."

"Gosh. I'm learning fast. And where are we now? There seem to be no traffic rules in the centre of the city? What's happening? Why so much noise? Is something wrong?"

"People just drive anywhere they like here, blowing their horns as loud as possible. They don't pay any attention to the rules of the road. There is no driving test. You just get a licence and drive if you know someone in the Traffic Department."

"Oh my word, that's incredible. But our taxi driver seems to be holding his own all right!"

The old Mercedes with its faded upholstery and battered

paintwork was ducking and diving through the traffic, the driver bent over the wheel as if he was in a pedal car. On the rear view mirror dangled a hand of Fatima and a Cedar of Lebanon swinging from side to side according to the movements of the car. It was with some relief that the taxi drew to a halt in a crowded street at the entrance to a small four-storey cement structure, evidently an apartment block. Nabeel paid the cab and got their small cases out.

"This is it. Let's go upstairs."

Rose followed him into a narrow stairwell and up to the second floor, where two doors gave onto the staircase. He rang the bell on one of the carved wooden doors. Joyful cries followed the peal of the bell.

"Ahlan wa sahlan, ahleen, wahashtini awi," cried the middle-aged woman who emerged first from the open door.

While Nabeel embraced her, Rose watched a series of children, aged from teens to tots, follow their mother, all smiling, some saying words of welcome. Rose wondered what she was supposed to do. She did not know any Arabic, so simply waited for her cue from Nabeel. He turned and spoke to her:

"This is my sister, Marie, and these are her children, my naughty nieces and nephews."

The last two appeared to be the same age. Rose found out later that they were indeed twins, aged four years while the oldest child was 16. Rose thought to herself this is definitely a Catholic family!

"Where's Younis?" asked Nabeel.

"At work, of course," Marie replied. "He'll be home for dinner at 8 o'clock. Come and have some refreshments now."

The cases and the couple were swept into the hall

corridor, and then to the sitting room, where cold drinks were served first.

"Cola or Seven Up?" enquired Marie.

"Coca Cola, please," replied Rose.

Marie and Nabeel laughed, while the children who were watching looked shocked.

"There's only Bibsi here," Nabeel mocked the Arab pronunciation which Rose knew about from her teaching. "Coca Cola is on the Arab Boycott list, for having a production plant in Israel. But we've got Pepsi instead."

"That's interesting. I'd no idea. Sorry." apologised Rose.

"That's OK. How could you know?" smiled Marie, bringing her a tall glass of cola with ice cubes. She placed a small dish of something small and brown which Rose did not recognise beside her glass and beside Nabeel's. She also brought a large glass ash-tray and put it on the coffee table with the drinks and small bowls.

Rose looked over at Nabeel enquiringly.

He explained. "These are pumpkin seeds. We eat them as a snack, just as you in Britain eat peanuts and crisps. They are very healthy. But they are tricky to eat until you know how."

He demonstrated the correct technique, putting a seed narrow end first, lengthwise between his upper and lower teeth, then biting gently on the shell, cracking the seed open, then bringing it into his mouth to separate the seed from the shell with his tongue, finally extracting and placing the empty shell in the ash tray with his fingers. The watching children laughed and reached out eagerly to continue the demonstration themselves.

Marie cried out "*La!* No! Not for you. It's nearly dinner time. You wait for your food."

The children sank back onto their cushions and stools disappointed, but not unhappy. They had been pushing their luck, they knew.

Rose turned to the smallest girl, and asked her in English, "What's your name?"

The little girl blushed, giggled and ran away. Her twin replied proudly on her behalf, pointing in the direction she had run off in:

"She Susie, and me Georgie."

"Very good, Jou Jou," cried Nabeel. "When I last saw you, at Christmas, you couldn't say your name properly. Well done!"

Jou Jou smiled calmly. His nickname had stuck even though his pronunciation had improved.

The older girls had disappeared into the kitchen, presumably to help Marie with the food, as appetising smells began to emanate from there.

"Can I help you?" called Rose, staying politely on her seat, in case she was not allowed in the kitchen.

"No, no, no. *La, la, la.* You are a visitor today. Perhaps tomorrow you can help me," said Marie.

As Rose and Nabeel sipped their cold drinks, and Rose began to practise eating *bizzer*, the door bell rang.

The twins ran to open the door, shouting, "*Baba, baba*".

Marie's husband, Younis, came in smiling, extending his hand in greeting to Rose, and warmly embracing Nabeel.

"*Ahlan wa sahlan, ahlan bikum,*" he exclaimed, "welcome to our house, *beetna beetkum,* our house is your house."

It was the first time Rose had heard these greetings, and she noted them for further discussion with Nabeel. She liked the sound of Arabic and determined to learn as much as she could from now on. Marie brought Younis a cold drink then returned to the kitchen, bringing serving dishes to the dining table now that her husband was home. The savoury smells were delicious and Rose looked forward to eating her first Arabic meal.

"Itfaddalu," called out Marie as she, and the two older daughters placed the last dishes on the table. "Come and sit down."

Once everyone was seated around the large table, Rose was surprised to note that an Arabic grace was said by one of the children, concluding with *"Baraka fikum."*

Dishes of delicious food were passed around, some new, some known to Rose. There was hummus decorated with olive oil and parsley leaves, *baba ghanoush* with a similar small pool of oil and pomegranate seeds decorating it, *tabbouleh* salad surrounded by fresh green cos lettuce leaves, as well as the main dish, which looked like chicken with onions, called *musakhan* and of course, a pile of freshly warmed pitta bread as well as a much thinner flat bread, almost like a crepe, which Rose had never had before.

"That's Iranian bread," Nabeel explained. "You can't get it fresh everywhere, but it's available here and delicious when warm."

There was also a plate of crunchy French fries, which were being devoured hungrily by the children.

"I made those especially for Rose as she's a vegetarian," cried Marie. *"Shwaye, shwaye, ya uwlaad.* Slowly, slowly, kids!"

"Thanks very much for this delicious meal," Rose replied. "There's plenty for me to eat, don't worry. By the way, how do I say delicious in Arabic?"

"Lazeez," replied the children almost in unison.

"*Lazeez,*" Rose repeated several times. "I like that word, and I love this food!"

After the meal Rose went into the kitchen with Marie and the older girls to help clean up. Marie was a capable housewife, who ran a tight ship. The girls began washing up using an enamel bowl with a small amount of hot water and powder Tide detergent for the first wash, then rinsing the dishes under the cold tap in the large rectangular sink. It was a new method for Rose who observed the process with interest as she dried the dishes. Marie put them away in the various cupboards. Noticing Rose's interest she explained:

"We pay a lot for electricity to heat the water, so we don't use a lot if we can manage. We take cold showers in the summer too to save money."

Rose realised that the flat was sparsely furnished, but clean and tidy. The tiled floor in both kitchen and living/dining room was swept and mopped after the meal, so that the place was comfortable to sit in. Nabeel and Younis had been talking and smoking while the women were in the kitchen. Rose looked at Nabeel's face. He seemed a little upset. She went to sit by him and asked quietly what was wrong.

"It's OK. I'll explain later," he told her. "We aren't going to stay here tonight. We're going to a flat in the downtown district. Younis has booked it for us. You'll like it."

"OK. There's probably no room here for us anyway."

After a cup of coffee, '*saada*' (no sugar) for Rose and '*helu*' (sweet) for Nabeel, and some more family talk catching up with the latest news from Kuwait, Rose and Nabeel picked up their bags and followed Younis to his rather battered car.

"It's a short drive downtown," he told them. "The district is called the Hamra - it means red."

"I hope it's not the red light area," Rose commented wryly.

"No, it's a very fashionable area, where tourists stay."

"I see," Rose noted she was a tourist, not family. Was this an insult or a special favour she wondered?

The evening air was cool and the city was dark as they drove through the streets. The traffic was minimal but the streets were not quiet as it was Saturday night. Even though it was now after ten o'clock and shops were closing, some cafes were still open, selling juices and roast chicken on the spit. The smell of garlic was in the air. They pulled in near a small, high-rise building which appeared more modern than the apartment block. With their cases they went into a lift and up to the fourth floor.

"You'll have a good view from here," Younis said as he opened the door and gave them the key. "Of course, you won't see it till morning. Come over for breakfast tomorrow. We'll have *manaeesh*!"

"*Tayyib*," said Nabeel. "We'll see you around 10. Is that OK?"

"*Tamaam*," said Younis as he raised his hand in farewell salute and left them to settle in.

"Thanks for everything," called Rose as he went out.

The room was spacious, with a large double bed covered with a burgundy bedspread. On closer inspection the bed was clean. There was a balcony and an *ensuite* shower and toilet. There was also an air-conditioning unit, something novel to Rose, and a fridge with two small bottles of mineral water inside.

"This seems fine," Rose said. "What was the problem earlier?"

"Well, it's the old customs here," he told her. "Because we are not married there would be gossip if we stayed with Marie. The children would not understand either. So it's best we are here."

"That's fine. No problem."

"The nice thing is we are downtown so we can go and see AUB and the Place des Martyres where my father used to have his tailor's shop. And I've got an old school friend who has a store on this street. We can visit him. It'll be great."

"OK. I'm going to have a shower and get ready for bed. I'll unpack tomorrow. I'm tired, aren't you?"

"Maybe one more cigarette...."

"Well, go out on the balcony please!"

"I know, I will."

After an eight hour flight and dinner with the family, Rose and Nabeel slept well that night.

The next day's sun was peeping through the blinds when they awoke.

"I could murder a cup of tea," said Rose. "Is there a kettle here?"

In fact they hadn't noticed the room had a kettle as well as an electric hotplate. There were plates and cups in the cupboard below it and some teabags, sugar, coffee and creamer sachets, so they could have a cup of tea while relaxing in bed.

"How will we get to Marie's?" asked Rose.

"We'll take a '*service*'. It's a taxi that takes a few people who are going in the same direction, so it's cheaper than a cab. That's how people get around the city. There aren't any local buses. We'll leave around 9.30am."

"OK. I'll unpack. It won't take long: I'll hang my dress in case I need it later in the week. Is it casual dress this morning?"

"Oh yes, not formal at all."

When they went out onto the street Rose was wearing her green flared trousers and her yellow short-sleeved knit top. She felt slim, clear-skinned and in holiday mood.

"Let's go into the store and get some sweets for the kids, shall we?" she suggested.

The supermarket across the street was one of those owned by Nabeel's friend, so greetings were exchanged and a message passed on to the proprietor that his old school friend was back. On arrival at Marie's home, the two boys were kicking a football around in the small yard around the building. The street was not empty, even though it was Sunday morning. To Rose this seemed unusual and she commented on the lack of a holiday atmosphere.

"Well, you know, this is a secular country. Not everyone is Christian. There is nothing exceptional in Sunday for Muslims. Their holy day is Friday and we Christians carry on our business on that day, while they go to the mosque."

"Does the family go to church, then, on Sundays?"

"Not here in Beirut. They go to church in Aijaltoun, up in the mountains, where they have a summer house. They usually spend weekends up there too, but they've stayed here to welcome us. We might be going up there after breakfast."

The boys led them upstairs and on entering the flat the smell of coffee wafted towards them, together with the warm smell of fresh bread.

"Mmm, that smell is *lazeez*," said Rose, remembering her Arabic lesson from the preceding night.

"It's *manaeesh*," explained Marie. "*Ahlan, itfaddalu*, come and sit down and eat. I've done the coffee for you the way you like it. Would you like some fresh orange juice?"

"That would be lovely," Rose gratefully accepted.

The dining table held a large bowl of boiled eggs, a plate of shiny red tomatoes, bright green spring onions and short fat Lebanese cucumbers. There were bowls of plump black and green olives, as well as a dish of creamy, thick, white yoghurt.

"This is *lubna*, it's a semi-dried yoghurt," explained Marie. "If you like yoghurt you'll love this."

There was also a pile of flat breads spread with glistening, green, first-press, virgin olive oil and a purple-coloured sprinkling of seeds.

"This is *manaeesh*. It's famous in Lebanon. It's flat bread, olive oil and *zaatar*, that's thyme, with s*umac* spice and sesame seeds mixed in to make it more tasty."

"I don't think we have *sumac* in Britain, but I love bread so I can't wait to taste this."

The family sat around the table and helped themselves to whichever of the breakfast foods they enjoyed most. Everyone had a whole piece of *manaeesh* and no one left any, though the twins shared a piece.

"This is so *lazeez*," cried Rose, making them all laugh. "It's a wonderful breakfast. And I love *lubna* as well as *manaeesh*."

"Good. You can have it every day. We eat *lubna* in sandwiches for lunch as well as breakfast."

"Now," said Younis, "we will show you some of Lebanon.

We are going to go to the house in Aijaltoun. We'll come back in the evening, OK?"

"That's terrific. Thank you so much."

Younis' car, they realised in daylight, was an old station wagon, which could take the four adults and the two youngest children on their knees. The older three children all stayed in the flat. They were going to the cinema matinee performance later.

"I'm sorry you can't come with us," Rose apologised.

"Don't worry, for us it's not worth driving up and down. We go there all the time," they explained in French.

They were not so comfortable in English with more challenging concepts.

"Oh, I nearly forgot, we brought you some sweets," Rose told them, digging into her large bag.

"Thank you, thank you. We'll take them to the cinema!"

"Don't eat them all," warned Marie. "You'll be sick and you'll get toothache."

Having cleaned up the kitchen and done the dishes, the travel party piled into the car and set off on the road out of Beirut to the north, towards Jounieh, a Christian town. The drive was interesting but the traffic was no more reassuring than it had been on the way from the airport. Drivers stuck to their side of the road, but veered off without any signals. It was a scary experience so Rose focussed on the deep blue sea to the left of them. On the right-hand side mountains began to appear and after about half an hour Younis left the motorway and headed up a steep minor road into the mountains. After another half an hour of twisting roads and small villages, surrounded by increasing numbers of pine trees, they eventually came to a small town, with stone-built houses and flat roofs.

"This is Aijaltoun," Younis proclaimed. "We've just finished building our house here."

He started up another much smaller road and eventually stopped outside a two-storey stone house.

"Our neighbours downstairs rent from us. We have the top floor and the roof. It's nice to sleep up there when it's hot in summer."

To Rose the simple structure looked delightful. There was the smell of juniper and pine in the warm summer air, and there were window boxes of flowers and herbs. The steps up to the first floor were covered with marble which lent some coolness to the interior, unlike cement which retains the heat. The door was heavy wood, carved ornately, which Younis opened proudly.

"Here we are: our summer residence."

He went inside, opening up the shutters at the windows to let in the breeze. There were countryside views all around, with a large building visible at a distance on the hillside, designed with huge arches.

"Is that a church?" asked Rose.

"Almost. It's a monastery. This area is Christian. You can hear church bells on Sunday mornings as well as for weddings and funerals. Come and have a look at the rest of the place."

They walked around four spacious bedrooms and a large kitchen. The open plan living room included a dining table and the whole apartment had marble floor tiles which were cool underfoot. The ceilings were high and there was a balcony running around three sides of the apartment, so that everyone could sit outside and enjoy the views.

"Who's for coffee?" asked Marie.

Everyone agreed it would be lovely to sit outside and relax with a drink. Rose noticed that neither Younis nor Nabeel smoked quite so much in this lovely mountain environment. Perhaps their lungs recognised a need for fresh air.

After coffee and discussion of the latest Lebanese politics Nabeel suggested they go up the mountain a little further to have a late lunch. It would be his treat. Marie looked at him gratefully. Clearly she appreciated a little respite from working in the kitchen. The Lebanese eat lunch late so the timing was appropriate. They got into the car again and drove through aromatic pine forest and up rocky hillsides. There were goats grazing below the trees, some with little collars and bells on them.

"Those are the leaders," Younis pointed out. "They know the way home. When night falls, they'll head back to their owners."

"How funny! They are really cute," cried Rose.

The car pulled into a large parking area near a low building surrounded by plants with an extensive outdoor patio covered with trellised grape vines. Bunches of grapes were already hanging in profusion.

"I didn't think they would grow at this altitude," Rose exclaimed.

"We get a lot of sunshine at the right time of year," explained Younis. "It's not difficult to grow them in sheltered areas."

Once in the restaurant, Nabeel ordered *arak*, the national drink, as an aperitif. Rose noted that Younis didn't refuse a drink even though he was driving, but he only took one glass during the whole meal.

"These restaurants specialize in grills," Nabeel explained. "That's the delicious smell from the barbecue. But you can also have grilled aubergines, halloumi and prawns, if you fancy them. We are not far from the sea even though we are up here in the mountains."

The usual *mezze* starters were brought, filling the table and giving the family something to nibble on while they awaited their mains. The shish kebab, *shish taouk,* and kofta kebabs arrived on large platters surrounded by crispy lettuce leaves and lemon halves. Rose had to try a little of each, despite her vegetarianism. The food was delicious. It tasted so fresh and smelled so interesting, flavoured with lots of onions and parsley.

"Now," said Marie, "here's something new for you." She proffered a small oval dish filled with a pale pink paste.

"What is it?" asked Rose, thinking it might be *taramasalata*, a Greek dish she loved.

"It's raw lamb, ground to a paste with cracked wheat and seasoned. We call it *kibbe naye.*"

"Oh, no," cried Rose in horror. "Sorry, but I can't possibly taste that. I'm a vegetarian, you know."

She watched in amazement as the others each took a spoonful, wrapped it in a lettuce leaf, sprinkled it with lemon juice and munched it with great enjoyment.

"You can only eat this in a place you know, because it would be unhealthy if it wasn't fresh," Marie explained.

A little faint with shock, Rose avoided looking at the dish until it was empty.

When all the serving dishes were cleared away, coffee

was ordered to taste for each adult. The children went off to play on the swings, slide and seesaw on the grass. The sunlight was warm but dappled with the shade of the vine leaves. It was an idyllic setting. Rose felt as if she was really on holiday in this completely new environment. Nabeel looked relieved at her obvious pleasure.

"What do you think you will do for the rest of the week," asked Younis. "Have you any plans?"

"Well, I'd like to take Rose to see Baalbek, Jaita, Tyre and Sidon, all those historic and beautiful places."

"You should be careful. There's been some trouble with the Palestinians and Israel in the south. Why not go north to Byblos and The Cedars instead?" suggested Younis. "And what about next weekend? Will you come back here? We'd like to spend some more time with you before you leave."

"Yes, I could book into the hotel here. That would be nice for Saturday night. I can't hire a car because my licence is out of date with being overseas for so many years. I didn't have time to renew it when Joseph was getting married."

There was a small silence at the mention of Joseph's marriage. It had not lasted. Rose did not know if it was the truth, but the story was that the bride had not been a virgin. After the wedding night Joseph had immediately left her and the marriage was annulled. According to Nabeel, girls who had had sex before marriage sometimes had an operation to repair the hymen so that future husbands would not be suspicious. Rose could only wonder at what had happened in Joseph's case.

Perhaps so as to change the subject Younis jumped in with a suggestion.

"You can come up here with me next Saturday morning.

I'll bring Marie and the children up here after work tomorrow, as they are on summer holidays you know. But I'll be your chauffeur next weekend. I'll take you back on Sunday afternoon, so you can get your plane on Monday."

"That's very kind of you," Nabeel said. "You've reminded me too that I have to confirm our tickets at the MEA office in the city centre, and I have to contact Charbel and his family. I might get to see my old friend Jean."

"You'll be very busy next week sightseeing and meeting people, so you can enjoy a relaxing weekend with us before you go back to London," Marie told Rose. "We can go up to the snowline if you like."

"That would be great. I've heard that you can swim and ski in the same day here in Lebanon," replied Rose.

"That's what the Tourism Office says, but most people prefer to do one or the other," laughed Marie.

By 4pm the sun had dimmed and the family decided to make their way back to Beirut. Younis dropped them at their building where they all embraced Lebanese style with three kisses on the cheeks, left hand side first.

"See you next weekend. *Maa salaamah!*"

The next day they made their plans over their morning cup of tea. They decided to look around the city later and perhaps see Jean if there was any contact from him. The following day they would make a long trip to the Roman ruins at Baalbek. Wednesday they would visit the ancient city of Byblos and the Cedars of Lebanon near Bicharre where Khalil Gibran was buried. Thursday they would try to see Charbel and Friday they would leave to chance, knowing they were going up to Aijaltoun again with Younis the next day.

They dressed for the sun as they would be walking around a fair amount, taking taxis for longer distances. One of the first places they headed to was Martyrs Square. The imposing entrance to the American University of Beirut was near here.

"Adel got his engineering degree here, didn't he?" asked Rose. "Where did you go to university?"

"Oh, I didn't go to university, that's why they sent me to England. I was a rebel at school. I couldn't think the way they wanted me to. When I wrote my answers in the baccalaureus exam, at the end of school, I didn't pass because I did my own thing."

Rose felt slightly uneasy when she heard this. Rule-breaking was not her style. "So how did your brothers feel about that? Did they support you while you were studying at school, too?"

"Yes, of course. I'm next to the youngest. They have to," he told her nonchalantly.

"But they must have been cross when you didn't get your qualifications," Rose remonstrated.

"I don't know. That's their problem. I just couldn't accept what the teachers were saying. They were *Freres Maristes*, Marist Brothers. They just wanted everyone to believe in religion and kiss the Bishop's hand when he visited. I refused to do that myself. He's only a man. He's not God."

"Well," said Rose, "I can understand that. I used to believe in God, and at one time, when I was very young, I thought I saw a vision in church when I was about twelve."

"Really? What kind of vision?"

"I sensed a presence in our old Saxon church, rather than saw a figure. It was Evensong, and we sat in the choir stalls. I

153

was looking at the priest as he gave his sermon in the pulpit. The church had oil lamps and there was a warm feeling in the air. Suddenly I felt overwhelmed with emotion, as if someone was speaking to me."

"What were they saying?"

"Take Jesus to the poor. Become a missionary."

"Do you think the priest was talking about that in his sermon?"

"Maybe. I can't remember. But anyway, I've got over it now. There's no way I would be a missionary, and I don't think I believe in God anymore. After you study science, religion seems like a fairy story."

"As Karl Marx said, religion is the opium of the people."

"I agree. Everyone needs a crutch to lean on, especially in hard times."

"Yes, and Catholics have hard times because they can't practice birth control, so they have too many kids. The Muslims too."

"Really? Birth control is against the religion?"

"Yes, indeed. The more kids the merrier. But talking about families, here is where my father had his tailor's shop. He was a merchant tailor, not one of those tailors who sit on the floor and sew by hand. He was an agent for various cloth companies, expensive ones, like Dormeuil, the French company."

"I know that name. That's interesting. But none of you followed in his footsteps."

"No way. It's not a business where you can make money. Contracting and trading are much more profitable. Now, are you ready for some brunch? I can see just the place."

They crossed the square to a cafe. There were tables on

the pavement where Nabeel selected a shady seat for Rose, while he went inside. When he came back, he told Rose what they were having.

"This cafe makes fabulous Lebanese cheesecake. I know you'll like it. Do you remember our first date? Our first meal together?"

"Yes, I had apple pie. So this is similar to fruit pie?"

"Not at all, but it's sweet!" As Nabeel was speaking a waiter came outside with two plates on each of which a bright orange square was resplendent. He brought glasses of water for them both and knives and forks.

Rose took her cutlery and investigated the cheesecake.

"It's like orange straw on top of melted cheese. Mmm, it's delicious."

"We call it *konafe*. It's *lazeez*, isn't it?" he smiled, gently mocking her first word in Arabic.

"It certainly is. Perfect for breakfast. It's a whole meal in itself."

After finishing their *konafe* they had a Turkish coffee, while Nabeel had a cigarette. They then continued their exploration of the city. The contrast of modern buildings with older ones was a surprise, but until 1975 when the Lebanese civil war started Beirut was still the Paris of the Middle East, with fashionable shops and people everywhere. The city was bustling.

That afternoon on returning to the hotel they found a message from Jean stuck to their door. He was inviting them for dinner. Rose was glad to be able to wear her glamorous cotton maxi dress. Jean invited them to his penthouse apartment above the supermarket across the street. It was very upmarket, with spacious open plan living areas with marble floors, many gilded floor-length mirrors and Murano glass pendant lamps. Above this floor was a rooftop garden furbished with varied pot plants and small palm trees in strategic positions. Jean introduced them to his wife, Nadia, and two other couples Nabeel had known when he was a student in Beirut. With his six guests seated on the elegant rattan furniture, Jean served drinks which were heavily iced, American style. For their first drink Rose and Nabeel enjoyed their favourite but very expensive in Lebanon, scotch on the rocks. Next, Jean urged them to try his own arak, made from his own grapes grown in the Bekaa Valley. He had his own vineyard brand, which he felt was stronger and better tasting than others. Rose agreed that it tasted delicious, but warned him:

"If this is your special drink which you treasure more than scotch, then I'd better stay with the scotch!"

The rest all laughed at this. Nabeel assured him his best arak would not be spared if it was left to Rose. Jean laughed heartily too, but placed the bottle back in its cupboard. As they nibbled on pistachios, olives and salted almonds Nadia and her Sri Lankan maid brought in a selection of dishes for dinner: prawn cocktails, with huge prawns on shredded lettuce and thousand islands dressing; smoked salmon with capers and lemon slices, accompanied by melba toast; *kibbe naye* which Rose studiously avoided; and vine leaves stuffed with rice and pine nuts in a lemon sauce. Then Jean went to the barbecue to grill steaks to everyone's taste.

Apologetically Rose explained she was a vegetarian. "But there's plenty for me to eat, no need to worry about it."

Nadia spoke to the maid who went out, returning

with a dish of sliced feta cheese, as well as platters of salad vegetables and warm pita bread.

"The cheese is for you, Rose," she said. "Some protein instead of the meat."

Thanking her profusely, Rose blushed a little. Obviously the Lebanese were excellent hosts as well as generous ones. Jean opened some wine which had come from his vineyard in Mount Lebanon. Both red and white varieties were delicious.

The conversation turned mainly on the past and events from the host and guests' youth, but politics was involved too. The high cost of living was mentioned, with the Lebanese pound worth very little, and people living on American dollars. There was a folk saying that there were more Lebanese abroad than living in Lebanon. These friends said it had been true now for many decades. More and more young people were seizing the chance to get out if they could.

All in all it was a very interesting evening for Rose. The female guests were elegantly dressed, with jewellery which obviously was expensive. Luckily the new dress Rose had made suited her slim figure very well.

"You were the prettiest girl there," Nabeel complimented her as they went back to their room.

"Thanks, darling. That's nice of you. I must say I enjoyed the evening. Jean speaks great English, doesn't he? I know all your friends do, but he seemed more fluent than the rest. I suppose it's because he's in business."

"Actually, it's because he had an English girlfriend for years. Her name was Janet. They say you learn a language best if you can have pillow talk in it. Jean studied in London like me."

"I see," commented Rose drily. "Is that why you picked me? You wanted to perfect your English?"

"Don't be silly."

"So what happened to Janet? Is she out of the picture now he's married? How did she take that?"

"Well, of course she was very upset, but she was older than Jean so she should have expected he wouldn't stay with her forever. We Arabs have to marry a much younger girl."

"Oh, so I'm OK, am I? My age won't rule me out if we get to that stage? You are seven years older than me, aren't you?"

"Yes, but that's not much here. Men can marry someone 20 or 25 years younger. That way they are wealthy and experienced. But women have to be young and fresh."

"... and virgins?"

"Indeed."

"OK. Let's close the subject. I'm never getting married anyway. I've seen enough of what sadness that can cause."

The arak and whisky together with the good food sent them off to sleep soundly.

The next day, Tuesday, Nabeel had booked a car and a driver/guide who spoke French to take them to see the Roman ruins of Baalbeck. The journey would take around an hour on the main road to Damascus. After the sightseeing they would visit the village of Zahle, famous for its *mezze*, an array of innumerable small dishes of many types of food, rather like a Spanish tapas multiplied by ten.

Baalbeck was amazing. The Corinthian columns were huge. The morning sun was getting warmer towards midday as they finished their tour and got back into the car. In Zahle there were lots of restaurants with tables lining the walls above what appeared to be a river. The sound of rushing water was so loud Rose could hardly hear herself think.

"Do we have to sit here?" she asked as they looked at the menus the waiter brought.

"This is the best place to sit. Arabs like the sound of running water. It's refreshing."

"I see, but it's also a bit too cold and rather dank. I'd rather sit in the sunshine under an umbrella."

"OK, we'll move," he agreed a little reluctantly.

As they were moving a poorly dressed pedlar approached them, his wares on a wooden tray held in front of him by a leather strap around his neck.

"Baaden, baaden," Nabeel muttered scowling.

"I hope you weren't nasty to him," said Rose.

"Not at all. I told him later, when we are settled again."

The man went on to show other customers his tray while Rose and Nabeel settled at a table away from the sound of water. They ordered soft drinks and Nabeel gave the waiter an order for a mezze for two people.

"We'll get a variety of small dishes you can choose from," he told her.

"I'm hungry, so I hope they are mostly vegetarian," she warned and started picking at the warm flat bread on their table. While they were sipping their drinks the pedlar returned and showed them a variety of small bejewelled knives, suitable as paper knives, and bangles and other inexpensive items of jewellery.

"Kam? How much?" asked Nabeel, holding up a couple of items Rose was interested in.

The pedlar gave a figure which seemed reasonable to Rose, but Nabeel immediately bargained him down to about half of the original price. Rose was cross.

"Why did you do that? He's a poor fellow, he needs the money."

"Yes, but here we can't pay the asking price, we have to bargain or we look like fools."

"But he probably thought you were a Westerner, and gave you his best price immediately, don't you think? With your pale skin you don't look like a local at all."

"Maybe, but he'll learn that he should expect even Westerners to bargain these days."

"Oh, you're so mean," Rose said in exasperation. "Don't you like helping people?"

"Not if it makes me look stupid. Anyway, you got your knives, so be happy."

"Thanks, but you spoilt it. There'll always be a nasty memory attached to them."

Rose was feeling increasingly hungry as well as irritated, but her bad mood lessened as the food started to appear. There were lots of items she was now familiar with: *hummus, mutabbel, tabboule, labneh*, vine leaves, *fattoush* salad, *kibbe* balls, olives, but also a few she had not seen before.

Nabeel identified a dish of lamb brain and another of intestines and moved them over to his side of the table. The other new dish was *falafel,* ground chick pea patties in a sesame seed, or *tahini*, sauce. Rose loved these. She added *falafel* to her mental directory of delicious Arabic dishes.

"Do you think this will be enough for us?" Nabeel asked. "Shall I order a grill?"

"No need. This is plenty for two of us at lunchtime. We won't be able to finish these, I'm sure."

After eating as much as they could, they set off back to Beirut, Rose's mood improved with the two decorative souvenir paper knives safely in her handbag.

That evening they both felt tired and needed an early night. They drank their duty free whisky on the rocks and ate a flat bread sandwich from a street cafe, lamb *shaworma* for Nabeel and *falafal* for Rose. As they munched contentedly they planned the next day's trip to Byblos and the magnificent Cedars of Lebanon.

The same driver/guide as the day before turned up at 9am promptly.

"He must think you are English or French," laughed Rose. "I didn't think Arabs were so punctual."

"He wants his money, that's all. I haven't paid him yet for yesterday."

"Oh no, that's not fair. Why on earth didn't you pay him yesterday?"

"I wanted to be sure he'd turn up today. And if I'd paid him yesterday he would have expected a tip. So if I pay him today, that will be one tip for two days."

"Oh my word, you are meaner and craftier than I thought," she retorted.

Rose's cheerful holiday mood was dimmed by yet another display of what she saw as tight-fistedness. She was a generous person and found it difficult to accept the cross cultural difference displayed despite the logical motive behind Nabeel's behaviour. She kept quiet, nevertheless, not wanting to spoil the atmosphere of today's trip.

"I see. Come on then, let's go. Have you got your camera?" she asked, changing the subject.

Nabeel's camera was a bit of a joke between them. As soon as he started travelling to France for his job he had surveyed the Duty Free camera shops at the airport. He had invested in a large leather camera bag, a professional quality Olympus camera with tripod, long lens and sharp focus, as well as a 360 degree lens. Rose was a keen 'snapper' for memories but not for art. Evidently Nabeel prided himself on his photographic skill. They joked about his camera bag's resemblance to a shoe-shine boy's kit. Shoe-shine boys were still working on Beirut's streets, so the joke was relevant. So far Rose had not seen any evidence of Nabeel's superior skill but this holiday would provide the opportunity for him to demonstrate it.

"Yes. All here, and lots of film. I must get the shots from yesterday developed before we leave. They do it well here and we can show the family. The kids will enjoy them."

On the journey eastward they passed the shambles of the refugee camp of Tel al Zaatar.

"I feel really sad when I think how these people have lived for the past 35 years."

"Me too, but Yasser Arafat will get something done soon, I hope. Did I tell you I was a fighter in Black September?"

"Yes, when I met you, and when I stayed that first night you showed me your 'fighting trousers' with the skull and crossbones inked on them. But were you serious? I thought you were joking."

Nabeel was able to avoid answering as they arrived in Bicharre and changed the subject.

That night the two were tired again after sightseeing

in the hot August sun. The next day they decided to set off for the beach on the Corniche. They took a service taxi to a luxury beachside hotel and paid a small fee to use the facilities, the beach beds, umbrellas and toilets and showers. Towels were not provided but they had brought their own. It was wonderful to relax with a book by the water, taking a refreshing dip now and then.

"I must get in touch with my old friend Charbel. He's an unusual person, but fun to be with. I asked Jean to get in touch with him. Let's call at the supermarket when we get back and see if he's found him."

They spent the whole day enjoying the sea breeze and the waves, having lunch and beers to refresh themselves. They took a nap under the shade of the umbrellas then showered and hailed a *service* back to Hamra Street. When they checked with Jean later, they got Charbel's number and called him. He insisted they come up to see him the next day.

Charbel lived in the Christian town of Jounieh, north of Beirut. They took a *wanette* up there and Charbel came down to pick them up in Jounieh's main square. Rose noted his pale skin, fine features and surprisingly blue eyes. He was tall and slender, like Nabeel, but much more handsome, Rose thought.

"Ahlan, ahleen, ahlan bikum," Charbel embraced Nabeel warmly, kissing him three times on the cheek. Turning to Rose he cried, "Who is this beautiful flower?"

Nabeel commented drily to Rose, "This is how you recognise a Lebanese, compared with a Palestinian. We are not flatterers."

"You mean you don't know how to treat a lady," Charbel

corrected with a grin. "We Lebanese believe ladies are charming, and we have to treat them in a charming manner."

Rose laughed. "Well I must say it is very nice for a change. I could get used to it."

"Come on, I've a surprise for you at home."

They piled into the car and drove up a steep, narrow, winding road to a large gateway whose gates were remotely controlled. After the gates came a long drive, until silhouetted above stood a three-storey house. On the facade there were what could only be described as gargoyles.

"Wow. This is different," said Rose.

"Different good, or bad?" asked Charbel.

"Different interesting," said Rose diplomatically.

"I made these myself. I'm very artistic," Charbel proclaimed without modesty.

Nabeel laughed. "Who told you that? It looks like kids' stuff. Are you sure you didn't get them from a toy shop?"

"Come on, you just don't appreciate unique things."

As they bantered the double front door opened and a young woman stepped out, holding a baby.

Nabeel's mouth dropped open in surprise.

"You're married?" he asked.

"Of course. Isn't it time you did the same?" Charbel smiled meaningfully at Rose.

"Mabruuk, congratulations. I had no idea. And who is this lovely little thing?" Nabeel asked, ignoring the comment.

"My wife, or my baby? This is Carmel, my lovely wife, and this is our daughter, Hope."

"What a lovely name for a lovely baby," complimented Rose.

"Welcome, Rose," said the young woman.

"Hello, nice to meet you, Carmel. I'm sorry we've come to visit you empty-handed."

"There's no need for formality," Charbel assured them. "We are old friends. *Beetna beetkum.* Our house is your house."

"Thank you so much," Rose said, feeling cross with Nabeel that he had not thought to bring even a bottle of wine for his old friend. She realised she would have to take a more proactive role in their social life here.

Charbel proudly showed them around the interior of the house.

"This is all my design," he said, indicating the mezzanine with its minstrel gallery balcony. "There are six bedrooms, because we often have family here. Carmel's family is from the Bekaa Valley."

The tour of the house over, Charbel got them all drinks, and led the way down a crazy-paving path to a promontory on the hill where they had a splendid view of the Corniche. There was a large wooden pergola providing shade for the fixed seating and a large table. Charbel and Nabeel carried out some cushions to place on the benches where they sat to enjoy their drinks.

"Well," said Nabeel, "you've chosen a wonderful place to build your house."

"This was my father's land, you know. So it was quite easy. All I had to do was find the money, supervise and put the finishing touches in."

Rose wondered how Charbel had found the money.

"What do you do, Charbel?" she asked.

"Oh, this and that," he prevaricated. Carmel said nothing, simply dandled the baby on her knee.

Nabeel was watching and made no comment. Rose wondered if he was jealous. It was quite obvious that Charbel had had a completely different upbringing as a pure Lebanese, and the son of a wealthy man. Now he had a beautiful house, wife and baby. It would not be surprising if Nabeel was envious after a childhood tinged with terror, grief at the loss of his mother, then moving to a new country and living as a refugee, eating tomato and rice soup twice a day. Chicken had been their weekly luxury, which explained the cry of 'Cocorico' when Rose had cooked that first lunch.

"I suppose the house and garden keep you busy," Rose suggested.

"Oh no, I've got a gardener. I enjoy being with the baby. Time flies. Wait until you've got one," he said with a smile.

This time it was Nabeel and Rose who avoided answering. After all, marriage wasn't on Rose's agenda at all, nor children.

The afternoon passed quickly with some delicious food cooked on the BBQ by Charbel: steaks for the men and slices of aubergine, courgette, red and green peppers and halloumi cheese grilled and seasoned with a rich olive oil and red wine vinaigrette for the women.

"I prefer to eat vegetables too," said Carmel. "But I usually have to cook meat for Charbel. Unless he goes fishing."

"Hey, that's an idea," Charbel shouted from over at the grill. "Let's go down to the Corniche after lunch and go in the boat. You can water ski, *mon ami*."

"Wow, that sounds wonderful, but we haven't brought our swimming costumes with us," explained Rose.

"Well, Nabeel can borrow a pair of my trunks, but I'm not sure about Carmel's bikini on you."

"I won't swim, thanks. I'll just enjoy watching Nabeel fall flat on his face."

Carmel declined the sea excursion in favour of an afternoon nap with the baby. In fact, when they got down to the speedboat moored at the marina, Nabeel demonstrated that he could water ski. Rose was amazed that he had the agility and the stamina given his chainsmoking habit. She had never seen him participate in any kind of sport. Even Charbel was impressed.

"We used to do it when we were kids, but I'm better at driving now than being on the water."

"It's amazingly beautiful here on the water," said Rose. "It's so lovely to be on a boat too. It's interesting to see the coastline from here. The villages look so Mediterranean clinging to the rocky surfaces of these mountains. And I can see some snow up on the summits."

"Perhaps we'll go up to the snowline at the weekend," Nabeel told her.

"Yes, go to Fakhra and Faraya, it's historic as well as sporty up there," Charbel urged.

When they'd worn themselves out on the boat, they said their farewells, turning down Charbel's offer to drive them into the city.

"No need, you should get back home, but it's been great to meet you," Rose thanked him as they embraced, Lebanese style with three cheek kisses.

"You've got some great friends," she told Nabeel as they waited for a *wannet*. "Don't they make you feel you want to be here instead of in London?"

"Not at all. It's a dead-end street here. The politics are quiet for the time being, but it's a bonfire waiting for a match. Kuwait would be better, but not yet for me."

At least, Rose thought, she'd got an idea of what plans were in his mind. She wondered if she figured in them at all. But for now, she was happy with another experience to write up in her diary.

Friday, the Muslim holy day, was notable for the Friday prayer 'sermon' being broadcast over speakers across the city. Rose had heard the *muezzin* echoing across the city five times a day, but as Hamra Street was mainly a Christian area, she had not been awakened by the *Fajr* (dawn) prayer. Today was different, lots of strident voices began preaching at around midday and continued for a good hour. They had decided to stay 'home' and do some laundry as they were heading for the mountain the next day. In the morning they had gone over to the Middle East Airlines office to confirm their tickets back to London. It had been another of those contrasting architectural experiences: old buildings next to modern tower blocks. They'd picked up *falafel* sandwiches and 'cocktail' juices for lunch. It was pleasant to relax for a change, Rose reading a French magazine and Nabeel sorting through his films and photographs.

The next day they were ready for Younis, who picked them up at 8.30am. They put their small weekend bag and the camera bag into the boot. They handed Younis a couple of carrier bags containing beer and red and white wine. They had put the whisky in their weekend bag.

"Are you going into the shoe shine business?" laughed Younis, observing the huge, brown leather, camera bag.

"I might," joked Nabeel. "Service industries are always needed I learned on my diploma course in London."

The topic of education triggered a reaction in Younis. Now looking serious Younis told them about his current problem with his older son, Elijah.

"He wants to be a doctor, but he won't be able to get into a medical school here. There aren't enough places, and it's a *wasta* system - you need a sharp elbow to push you into the schools. A poor boy from a *phalistini lubnaani* family will not make it. I want him to follow me in the machine shop. I have a good business, my workshop is never short of work and if he learns to use the lathe and weld, then he'll have skills he can use for a lifetime. I really need him to follow in my footsteps, as we say in Arabic."

"We say that in English too. How much longer has he got at school?" Rose asked.

"Well, that's the thing. He could leave now, but he wants to stay on and get his qualifications for Uni. But it's expensive. I can't afford to keep six kids at school till they are 18. Helene and Diane have stayed on, because I don't want them to get married early. Helene is going to start architecture next year, and Diane is thinking of doing business. I want them to have a career as well as a family."

It was difficult to know what to say. Rose, of course, believed that Elijah should be given the same chance as his older sisters, but it wasn't her family, so she kept her mouth shut. Later, though, they discussed how they could help. Nabeel couldn't yet afford to help Elijah out, but he determined to do so in future.

When they got to Aijaltoun they first went to the Monte

Bello Hotel to sign in and leave their weekend bag. At the house Marie and all the children came out to welcome them.

"It's so nice to see you again, *wahashtuna* - we missed you! Come and have brunch, it's all prepared for you."

Rose and Nabeel sat at the table with the family and enjoyed the spread of dishes, including a new savoury tartlet called *sambosek*.

"It's vegetarian, with potatoes, peas and spices," explained Marie, cutting one open to illustrate the ingredients.

"Mmm, it's a little bit like Indian food," Rose commented.

"Yes, it is. Maybe we stole it from them. Do you like Indian food?" Marie asked.

Rose thought it best to simply nod rather than go into the details of how much Indian cuisine she had learned in her uni days. She recalled the tasty samosas she and Ramadas had bought a few times from the kebab shop.

Instead she asked, "Do people here eat a lot of Indian food? It's very popular in England. Some people say our national dish is butter chicken!"

A look of incomprehension passed over the faces round the table.

"Isn't roast beef the traditional English dish?" asked Younis.

"With those puddings from Yorkshire," added Nabeel laughing. "Don't worry Younis, it's a joke. It just means that's what so many people eat."

Relief dawned, and everyone laughed.

After lunch they all piled into the car and went up the mountain to the snowline. Farayah, they told Rose, had some ancient Roman ruins with pillars similar to those at Baalbek, but on a much smaller scale. The stone houses got smaller as they climbed higher into the mountains. Eventually they came to the snow and the children insisted on getting out and having a snowball fight. Rose, dressed for the summer rather than the winter, stayed in the car.

"I'm not keen on snow," she told them. "We used to get a lot when I was a child in England, and I always had chilblains on my feet."

"Chilblains?" asked the girls.

"I don't know how to describe them. They come when you get very cold. They are not infectious and there's no medicine for them. You just have to get warm and they go away," Rose explained. "I prefer hot weather and lots of sunshine."

"So you will love Lebanon, Rose. You must come and live here when you get married!" cried the oldest daughter.

Rose smilingly declined to respond, preferring not to enter into this topic, even though the family was obviously interested in the status of their relationship.

At this point, Younis suggested they drive on to the ski resort where they could have hot chocolate or icecream. When they reached Fakhra no one was skiing, as the piste was not open. Rose was surprised at the level of organisation for skiers, with a chairlift and a ski hire shop as well as hotels and cafes, though not many were open in the August low season.

"Well, we'd better start back," said Younis after their refreshment break. "At least you can say you know people can ski in the morning and swim in the afternoon."

"But we're not going swimming now, are we?"

"No, we're going to have some supper, the leftovers from lunch and just some simple food, flat bread with melted cheese and pickles, OK?" asked Marie.

"That sounds like the comfort food I love. We can drink some of the red wine we brought for you," Rose suggested. She had been surprised that no wine or beer had been served at lunch time. She wondered if it was impolite to mention it, but personally she enjoyed food much more when there was drink to accompany it. And drink didn't include cola!

"Of course, we forgot at lunchtime," said Marie, picking up her cue faultlessly. "We don't drink much as a family, just some arak sometimes, or a beer."

Rose felt relieved for two reasons: First, that Marie hadn't taken her comment as an insult, and second, that she would be getting a drink that evening. Although they had brought their duty free whisky for a hotel room night-cap, she had expected to enjoy a glass of Ksara that day!

Once back at the house the girls went into the kitchen to help Marie, while Rose sat with the littlest child on her knee. Rose was wearing a gold Arab puzzle ring which Nabeel had given her. The little girl pulled it off her finger in a moment of inattention by Rose. The ring fell apart and the little girl, dismayed, began to cry.

"What's wrong, *cherie*?" asked Rose.

"Maksour, maksour," cried the little girl bitterly.

Nabeel was ready to translate but Rose stopped him. "She said 'broken', didn't she? I can tell what she means by the situation."

"Yes, broken. Clever girl."

"I love learning languages. She said it so clearly too. I'll never forget that word."

Laughing, Nabeel put the ring together again and back on Rose's finger. The little girl stopped crying, staring at the 'unbroken' ring in amazement. The rest of the family were now placing hot food on the table. The older girls looked enquiringly at the ring, obviously wondering about its significance but Rose simply smiled and asked about a dish of brightly coloured vegetables she hadn't seen before.

"Those are pickled vegetables, turnip, carrot. We use a food dye to brighten up their appearance."

"Oh, I see. Makeup for vegetables, hey?"

Everyone laughed as they sat down again to help themselves.

"El akl al Arabi lazeez," stated Rose. "I learned a whole sentence. Arabic food is delicious."

Everyone laughed even more.

"Sahteen," shouted Younis. "Let's try our Lebanese red wine now."

He poured the rich, ruby-coloured wine into the adults' glasses. It was delicious and Rose's meal was complete. After a long, relaxed dinner Nabeel and Rose retired for the rest of the evening to the hotel. Elijah drove them, having just passed his driving test at 16 years old.

"You aren't afraid of my driving, I hope?" he asked.

"Not at all. I'm sure you know what you are doing," his uncle assured him. "Can you talk and drive at the same time?" he joked.

"Yes, of course. Why?"

"Well, I was wondering how school was going and if you had any plans for the future."

"I guess you've been talking to Dad, haven't you?"

"Not really. He just said he wants you to follow him into the machine shop."

"That's the problem. I don't want to do that. I want to be a doctor. I've seen so much violence here and although I appreciate the politics I don't think violence is the answer. I want to have Palestine as my homeland as much as anyone else, but I don't think we'll achieve it by fighting. So I want to heal people who get caught up in it."

"That's admirable," said Nabeel. "I'd like to help you achieve your ambition, but I'm not well-established yet myself. But I'll talk to your uncles and see if we can support you while you stay on at school, like your sisters. How does that sound?"

"It sounds great, thanks very much, uncle. Dad really doesn't want me to go back to school in September, but I want to go to university."

"OK. Well, keep it quiet for now, and I'll stay in touch with you."

Elijah smiled with relief and happiness. Rose hoped that Nabeel was being pragmatic as well as sincere in his promises. She had no doubt that he wanted to help his nephew, but she wondered how Nabeel's brothers would feel. After all, they'd only just finished supporting their younger brother financially

"See you tomorrow morning. I'll come and get you for breakfast - *manaeesh* as usual, Rose!"

"Maa Salaamah. Take it easy on the road, nephew."

The Monte Bello Hotel was a pretty, stone, three-storey building, with a large balcony from which there was an extensive view down to the coast. The room was cool, clean and simply furnished with its own *ensuite.*

"Would you like a nightcap?" asked Rose. "There's no ice, but we can have a splash of water."

Looking out through the window on the already darkened mountain, stars were beginning to appear in the sky. As they sipped their drinks they realised how still and quiet the night was. The next morning they were awakened first by the sound of cocks crowing, then by church bells. It made her happy but slightly homesick. She suddenly realised she had to send a postcard to Mum.

"Can we stop and get some postcards of the village on the way to breakfast?" she asked.

"Of course. Why don't we walk over? I'll give them a ring and tell them not to come for us."

The next day they walked to the village shops, then up to the house. Aijaltoun's houses were pretty with flowers in pots at the windows and doors, but the little stone church, whose bells they had heard, had a service going on so they did not go inside. After their walk they were ready for the appetising breakfast waiting for them in the house.

"After breakfast we're going to prepare *mulokhia* for lunch. It takes ages, so it'll be good to have another pair of hands," Marie told Rose.

Rose realised that the women's place was definitely in the kitchen as they cleared the table while the men set up a game of cards. Rose soon learned that *mulokhia* was a dark green, leafy vegetable, similar to spinach, which was stewed into a viscous soup and served with poached chicken. Picking the hard stems of each leaf out was the major task, but with four females in the kitchen the job was soon done.

"Time for an *aperitif*," said Younis, pouring large glasses of the now chilled white wine Nabeel and Rose had brought with them, to Rose's great satisfaction.

After another long meal they were ready to go back to the Monte Bello to check out, while Younis waited in the foyer to drive them back to Beirut. The farewells at the house had been effusive but Rose wondered if she would ever see any of the family again. The next day they were up early to complete their packing and get to the airport. After making some purchases with their remaining Lebanese *lire*, the two sat down with a beer to review the past two weeks.

"It's been so nice to meet the rest of your family and some of your friends. I've learned a lot about life here and a little of the language too. Thanks for bringing me."

"I think the family liked you. It's hard for them, you being British, but they don't blame you."

"I hope not. I was only a baby when Israel was created."

"Yes, it's not personal."

"Younis and Marie seem happy together. Why didn't Asma get married, do you know?" Rose dared to ask.

"Well, Asma has always been our little mother, plus, she only wanted to marry a doctor, an engineer or a lawyer, someone with professional status, not a tradesperson like Younis."

"Wow. But Marie accepted him?"

"Of course. He's a nice, reliable guy."

"But what about his son? Do you think he'll have to go into the machine shop?"

"I can't be sure yet, but I'm going to do my best to help him."

"That's great. He seems a very well meaning young man."

Rose wondered what would happen next, but for now, her happy holiday was over.

16

Lecturer 1, Adult Education, London

THE TRIP TO Lebanon had been revelatory in many ways, but in particular, she was glad that she had seen more of Nabeel's family and their way of life. What she did not know was that Asma had strongly objected to the visit and had quarreled with Nabeel on the phone. Once back in London the holiday soon faded in Rose's mind as she started her new job as fulltime Lecturer 1 in the AEI where she had worked part-time for a year.

The fulltime position from September was a step up for Rose. Not only did she have a department of around 40 part-time teachers in four locations to recruit and manage, and a daytime and evening curriculum to design and write placement and achievement assessments for, but she was to report to the Head of Training at the central London AEI to set up a schedule for training ESOL teachers on a part-time evening program. This involved Rose in lots more preparation. The program was needed as at the time there were only courses provided by International House and Garnett College. As usual Rose immersed herself in her reading and materials development. She found various new texts and planned a series of lectures. Although she was terrified, at the first session she met a young woman with stunning, long, auburn hair who became her friend and chief supporter. There were young people from BBC Teaching English on the course too. Rose was amazed to think they needed her input, but English Language Teaching was in its infancy in the '70s so trainers were in demand. She did the best she could, involving the participants in pair and group work and thinking on her feet as fast as possible to make the sessions fun. She did this course a couple more times but was relieved when the Royal Society of Arts Examinations Board developed CTEFLA courses in several main cities, so *ad hoc* courses like Rose's were no longer needed.

However, Rose's training skills were not curtailed, since another need was identified for volunteers to help with the UK Literacy Project. Rose met the challenge and trained volunteers in her own AEI as well as spent time and money on materials which tutors could use to help individuals. A new materials project for teaching immigrants called SCOPE was being developed at the time and Rose was keen to ensure she was keeping up to speed with developments in the field. Over the next year Rose developed the ESOL and Literacy programs offered by her AEI in the premises of day-schools in North London on which she taught herself. There were morning, afternoon and evening classes, the latter being the most popular with immigrants and residents who were working in the daytime. With the help of the other teachers she set up social events such as end of term parties and she led coach trips to places like Stratford on Avon, and to local theaters, museums and art galleries.

Rose witnessed many successes amongst the students and befriended several of them, such as Daisy, a West Indian origin immigrant who had come over in the '50s and still missed Jamaica, but regarded North London as her home. She worked as a traffic warden and had sole care of one teenage son. She never complained about the fact that her husband had left her, rather she was grateful she did not have to put up with his drinking any longer. Other friends were Carla from Colombia, visiting the UK for six months and Solomon, a young West Indian man who worked at the Ford Motor Factory in the East End of London but came to classes after work in his home area.

The need to keep accurate records of student attendance was emphasised in her part-time work with immigrants when a short, corpulent, middle-aged Turkish man was the subject of a police investigation. The administrative assistants were keen to keep small classes open, which depended on the ratio of staff to students, so they sometimes augmented the attendance record. Rose instructed them never to do so again when she was interviewed by the police about a particular date when a murder had taken place at the man's home address. His alibi was his attendance in class! Fortunately Rose kept her own records as her students were so diverse, she needed to log which individual worksheets each had completed in every lesson.

Now she was responsible for her staff, who afforded some challenges. Working late evenings ate into all the staff's social lives but one supervisor kept a bottle of gin in her bottom desk drawer and some tonic in the shared fridge to alleviate the pressure of work. A Welsh teacher of retirement age was lively and attractive with a thick mane of white hair but his story-telling teaching style was not student-centered. Rose was reluctant to spoil his fun but asked him to get the students to tell some tales of their own, with him listening and correcting appropriately.

As well as staff monitoring and development, teacher recruitment was demanding. There were not many fulltime ESOL jobs available in the UK so part-time work provided the main income for some. Reliable employers were the government AEIs and private schools organised under the ARELS (Association of Recognised English Language Schools) banner. Other schools operated with minimal standards and wages, so the AEIs were popular, even if the work was mainly evening 'unsocial hours'. One young man sometimes had to bring to class his baby, sleeping in a pushchair from 7.30 to 9.30pm. It wasn't ideal, but Rose felt she needed to support her staff provided they did their job well.

Another teacher's fate reminded her that life is not fair. Before the holiday, recruiting for the coming academic year, Rose appointed a good-looking young man, well dressed but with a mop of thick, unruly hair. When he failed to turn up for the staff orientation meeting in September, she contacted his address. His girlfriend tearfully explained that he had passed away. He had been suffering from cancer, and had been wearing a wig when Rose met him. She recalled her own serious illness in France. In London's winter, with her busy life and poor eating she frequently fell ill with flu and laryngitis. Her doctor suggested a tonsillectomy but she was also having dental treatment so could not spare the time off work.

After only one fulltime year as Head, the AEI Principal

decided to upgrade the position of Lecturer from Scale 1 to 2 on consideration of the huge number of ESOL students attending classes. This was a compliment to Rose for her work over the past year but of course the position had to be open to outside competition. Rose was shortlisted for the job and interviewed again by the friendly inspector. She was in a difficult position as she was also selected for the interview board for the other candidates, being the incumbent in the Lecturer 1 position. With this in mind she selected her clothes carefully: For the recruitment board she wore a sleeveless dress, but for the interview she put on the matching jacket so as to create a new persona. The interview went well, and she was promoted for her second year as Head.

17

Lecturer 2, Adult Education

AFTER HER FIRST year as Head of Department, she celebrated her success by taking Mum and John on a package holiday to Spain. Mum was suffering terribly now from RA and was moving to a disabled person's apartment as she could no longer manage the stairs at the three-storey house. After a horrific visit to the vet when Rose had to take John's cat *Minou* to be euthanased, as he was becoming a trip hazard for Mum, the holiday was a rare treat. Mum enjoyed eating paella for lunch on a visit to Barcelona, taking a boat trip, and drinking ice cold beer in a cafe on the beach. John showed off his skills in the swimming pool, diving for lost coins and jewellery. Rose was pleased she could now help her family a little more.

In her second year as Head of Department Rose continued the work she had started with some new additions to her own portfolio. The first was an extension to her teaching. She held a French class once a week attended by half a dozen 'old age pensioners' as senior citizens were called in the '70s. The audio visual (AV) technician was happy to fund some new technology for her class: a projector and slides which accompanied the course book. Some of the classrooms needed blackout curtains, so Rose and the AV officer made blinds with heavy black canvas and rope to haul them up and down. The students enjoyed the course which culminated in a trip to Paris. Rose booked cheap hovercraft Channel crossings and a small hotel for three older ladies and herself for the weekend in France. The quartet had a lot of fun, despite the age gap, and after shopping in Montmartre, Rose brought back a small copy of the Rodin statue, *The Thinker* for Nabeel.

Another new project was the 'Over 50s Club'. The attendees were young at heart even if over 70 in reality. One kind lady gave Rose a brass bell to help her get the attention of the rowdy group! She was responsible for arranging speakers, and excursions, and getting supplies for the tea break. Each member paid five pence for a cuppa and a biscuit. One highlight of the visits the 'Over 50s' group made was to the Guinness Brewery in North London, where Rose purchased some engraved mugs and pint glasses. But the star of the year was the matinee performance of Agatha Christie's *The Mousetrap*. As the audience were watching, engrossed in the plot, a small mouse crept onto the stage from the left hand side wings. A cry went up from the audience, "There's a mouse!" Peals of loud hysterical laughter followed. The mouse took fright at the noise and ran back to the wings. It was a fun anecdote for quite a while.

Rose still had to travel to several outlying school premises to teach evening classes. In fact, her official office was in a modern secondary school. It was only a place to file materials and use the phone but walking there from the bus stop she would pass a local Jewish bakery. The smell of the bread and pastries was enticing. She simply had to buy two pastries each time, scoffing them as she walked along the street. Her weight gain or loss was still an obsession in her diary entries, with daily and average monthly calorie counts, but she needed the energy to keep going, she told herself. Rose's diet probably lacked proper nutrition, which would account for her continued compulsive eating. And she was taking the contraceptive pill, which was known to affect hormone levels, so could have contributed to her changing moods as well as her weight fluctuation, which often triggered the petty arguments with Nabeel.

Meanwhile Nabeel was doing well working at the French steel company. He often travelled to France, Belgium and Italy so was improving his marketing and linguistic skills. He also frequently brought friends home and expected Rose to cook for them and him. His cooking skills were mostly demonstrated for occasional large parties. In light of their success they felt they could settle into a better home than the tiny bedsitter studios they both occupied. So after a tip off from a friend all their possessions were transferred from the bedsitters in Gloucester Road to a rented garden basement flat in Baron's Court. They took the plunge to move in as a couple, despite the arguments they continued to have from time to time over trivial issues. The flat had one large bedroom at the front below street level, a long, wide hallway leading to a bathroom, a large living room with a view up to the walled back garden and a small kitchen. The toilet was reached from the kitchen across a covered porch!

Rose recruited some Japanese friends from school to paint the flat white one weekend, fuelled by takeaway fish and chips. Mum gave Rose some of the furniture from the house, which would not fit her new disabled person's flat. The upright piano fitted nicely into the hall. The couple bought a new sofa bed and a rocking chair from the upmarket furniture store, Heal's, for the living room. Upholstered in fashionable Dralon these items coordinated well with the beige and brown abstract wallpaper. They bought turf and carried it through the hall to the garden where they laid it to form a small but lush lawn. Over the next months Nabeel constructed a barbecue out of brick with a forged-steel grill and drip tray which they used occasionally when the weather was good. Living here felt more like a permanent home, so Rose was content. Her job was going very well and she was not seeking a change.

However, living in London was challenging in the '70s on account of the bombings carried out both by the Provisional IRA (Irish Republican Army) and the PFLP. Once Rose's bus from the Midlands was held up on the road for two hours after the Hilton Hotel was bombed. Then, when she was conducting Friday afternoon student visits to places like the Stock Exchange, the British Museum and the Tower of London, she was always on edge in case they would be unlucky and become victims. When buying books for students at Foyles she was particularly vulnerable. All garbage bins had been removed from central London to prevent them being used as receptacles for bombs. In addition, the National Union of Mineworkers had held national strikes in 1972 and 1974 which caused the '3 Day Week' for workers. Evening institute classes were cancelled a few times on account of power cuts.

Nevertheless, feeling financially comfortable with her promotion Rose continued helping Mum financially and visiting Mum and John often, travelling by cheap coach or more expensive train when time was short. Life was sweet, she felt. She was climbing the career ladder and she had time and money to help her family. She and Nabeel did not always see eye to eye but they got on well enough. Sexually she now felt comfortable with him, but was not sure about his predilection for the soft porn videos which were popular at the time. '60s Free Love had given way to the Swinging '70s. Women's magazines such as Cosmopolitan were full of advice on how to satisfy your man, while feminists were propounding women's independence theories and burning bras. Rose's basic philosophy was modified. She had given up on her 'no sex before marriage' principle because she was not going to get married. The limited experience of sex she had to date had not impressed her, so that was that.

18

Diploma in TESOL

AFTER THE SECOND year as Head of Department Rose and Nabeel took Mum and John to Spain again for a summer holiday because the sunshine was so good for Mum's joints. On their return to the UK there was a bit of a scare when Nabeel was questioned by UK immigration. They suspected him of being Carlos the Jackal, a PFLP member who was wanted for international terrorism. Despite Nabeel's claims to have taken part in Black September when Rose first met him, he was cleared and allowed to leave, though they had missed their connecting flight to the Midlands.

On return from holiday Nabeel resigned from his French steel company job and left for Kuwait with the intention of working with his brothers and making his fortune, after serving his apprenticeship as a salaried marketing executive in Europe. His aim was to set himself up as a commission agent for companies whose products were required in Kuwait, serving the petrochemical industry in particular. His practical commercial experience selling French forged-steel pipes, valves and flanges would be invaluable to the purchasing departments of the oil industry. Rose reminded him that they were independent individuals and Nabeel should decide for himself if he wished to maintain their relationship. Over the past five years they had had various confrontations, and Rose was uncertain whether Nabeel was suited to be her life partner. In fact, she had always felt, since witnessing the arguments and tears of her father in the trauma of her parents' separation that she would never marry. She enjoyed being with someone but she did not want to be tied. Marriage was a cage she did not want to enter.

She was also busy at work. In her third year as Head of Department the Royal Society of Arts (RSA) began the pilot delivery of a a new TESOL course for teachers who were involved in teaching immigrants but who had no formal qualifications. It was taught at Westminster College in the heart of Soho. Rose secured permission from her boss to take the course. Course meetings were only one morning a week, so it was easy for Rose to fit into her mainly afternoon and evening work schedule. She needed a qualification for her own career development, so was glad of this opportunity.

After Nabeel left, Rose was happy in the garden flat, paying the full rent. She was now well established in her third year as Head of the English Department. The day-school where she spent most of her time was old and had the outward appearance of the traditional city school, with brick facades and huge windows made up of small, square panes of glass. The school caretaker was an older man with a beautiful Italian wife and two children, living in the school gate-house. The family became her friends because most of the teaching staff were part-time so Rose was quite isolated socially. Also the work was quite arduous, since the day was long. She did not know it then, but twelve-hour days were to become her normal work routine for the rest of her life. There were morning classes from 10 to 12, afternoon classes from 2 to 4pm and evening classes from 7pm to 9pm. Rose was in the building from start to finish, although her 40 part-time teachers came and went according to their schedule. She was inevitably tired after her long days, and she was studying as well, with practical assessments and essays to complete.

Rose's daily routine was simple. Each morning she took the Piccadilly Line to North London, where she popped into a corner shop to buy an 8oz slab of cheddar cheese. At work she divided this into two portions: one for lunch, one for 'tea'. She drank instant coffee and tea throughout the day and ate a couple of apples. At around 10pm back home, she had a scotch to relax before a bath and bed. In retrospect, the continual skin and digestive complaints and attacks of neurosis requiring her to take sleeping tablets were probably a result of stress and a poor diet. Also, the ongoing dental treatment was painful and tiring.

At weekends her routine included cleaning and laundry, shopping for fruit and vegetables on North End Road street market, and catching up with Mum and John. She heard from Nabeel occasionally, re-reading his letters often when she was free. He was doing well in the business world but there was little romance in his correspondence. She felt quite separate from him, especially when the flat was burgled and the Over 50's tea money stored in her wardrobe was stolen, as well as money from the electricity meter. She had to make good the amount stolen which she had recorded in an account book but that was nothing compared with the scared feeling and the loneliness she felt alone in the flat at night from then on. She had wanted to insure the place, but Nabeel had objected, saying it was unnecessary. Evidently it was, so she got it herself.

Rose, mulling over the past five and a half years together, had her doubts about their sex life. She did not find it particularly exciting, the thrill of dopamine was not there, nor had it ever been. Their physical unions were instigated by him and generated oxytocin for Rose, making her feel wanted and secure, but there was no passion on her side. So she was surprised when one weekday afternoon, she experienced a thrill which she had not felt since Alex. She had noticed a sale in a local dress shop, and went to investigate at lunchtime as she loved a bargain. By chance, the owner of the shop, a tall, handsome, dark-haired man, was checking on business with his shop assistant. A little banter followed and a date was made for a casual drink after class later that week. Rose was shocked at her own daring, agreeing to meet a stranger for a drink but a subconscious urge was waiting to be fulfilled.

The 9pm drink appointment which Rose had expected to be in a local pub turned into a somewhat undignified but definitely exciting encounter, drinking champagne in the shuttered shop storeroom/office. The thrill she experienced made her happy to accept an invitation to dinner near her home for a second date. When X arrived at her flat to pick her up in his Jaguar, she invited him in for a drink. However, the revelation that X was married compelled Rose to end the brief encounter there and then. She had no regrets but this experiment had proved the lack of sexual chemistry with Nabeel. Nevertheless, she asked herself how important sex was, given the length of time they had spent together and the other compatible aspects of their relationship so far. Rose now felt her biological clock ticking: She was 28 and beginning to feel she would like children. Marriage was the best environment to bring them up and Nabeel had proved himself to be a hard worker. Perhaps they were meant to be together, despite their disparate personalities and different cultural origins. Had fate played a hand in their meeting, after those initial words, "Can I help you?"

19

The Proposal

ONLY A FEW months after leaving the UK, Nabeel unexpectedly returned. He blurted out a surprising question almost as soon as he got into the flat. "Will you marry me?" He was so excited with his mission that he left his briefcase outside the front door. Because the front door was down a flight of stairs, unseen from the road the case containing duty free whisky and gifts was still there the next morning! Rose was so taken aback by this proposal that instead of answering she asked a question herself: "Have you forgotten our rows? This is me, not some dream girl." She wondered if it was a case of absence makes the heart grow fonder. Clearly life in Kuwait as a single man had not been very satisfactory if Nabeel wanted to take her back as his bride. And that was another reason for Rose to be amazed by the question. This was her third year in her new job which she loved. Was she willing to give her career up now?

Rose calmed Nabeel down with delaying tactics. She suggested that they both take six months to think about it. If she agreed to marry him after six months, she would be able to give the requisite three months' notice to her boss.

To boost Nabeel's morale they decided to go to the Playboy Club, still using Joseph's membership card, to celebrate their tentative engagement. Nabeel had brought with him a diamond ring, in a style he already knew Rose loved, with four bands of gold and a small diamond in the centre of each band. Fatefully it fitted, and Rose wore it with a sense of trepidation in her stomach. The photo taken that night in their flat shows Rose with an upstyled hairdo and an elegant white maxi dress and shawl, seated in the rocking chair from Heals, which Nabeel was most proud of.

The next day they travelled by coach to share the news with Mum and John, who both seemed pleased. Nevertheless Rose reminded Nabeel that her final decision was not yet made. She needed time to think. She had six months to decide whether to resign in May and leave her job in August. Particularly worrying was her concern that they did not have strong sexual chemistry. Sex was predictable after five years together, rather than exciting. She was not sure whether that was enough. Was this the right basis for a marriage? Could she even visualise herself in a marriage? She recalled the dancing Cinderella doll with her removable prince. She would be giving up her independence and moving to live in a culture she did not know. Religion was another concern. She wondered if Nabeel expected to marry in the Church, because she was not willing to convert to Catholicism with its doctrine of hell fire and mortal sin.

Nabeel stayed over Christmas which was spent at Mum's, with New Year and Mum's birthday celebrations. Mum was chronologically still a young woman, but her physical disability was increasing every year. Having retrained, she now worked as a book keeper/accountant in a hosiery factory. She had to take a bus to work each day, and life was getting more and more difficult for her. Rose wondered how she could accept a marriage proposal which would take her away from her disabled mother. The two of them discussed the issue and Mum was adamant that Rose should live the life she wanted to live. Her young son, John, would be with her for several more years, until he left school at least. Bill, now living and working in London, would be able to help out as required, so Mum urged Rose to simply think of herself.

She offered to read the Tarot Cards for her daughter. She had done this once before and the cards predicted career success. Rose did not believe in the power of Tarot but she was ready to take on board any help with her decision so she went along with the reading. The outcome this time, perhaps as a result of Mum's subconscious wishes, forecast domestic bliss. Perhaps Mum wanted grandchildren. Rose had to admit that she would like children, and she acknowledged that Nabeel was a hard worker. Together they could have a good life in which children would be an added blessing. So, weighing up the pros and cons logically, the deciding factor was that the world was their oyster. Together they could go anywhere, do anything, succeed in life materially and start a family.

Dad, when informed, also gave positive support. Rose realised there would be a problem at the wedding ceremony since her Mum and Dad had not met since their divorce. She would have to plan a different farewell for Dad's family. But for now, having celebrated Christmas and New Year, they returned to London. Rose saw Nabeel off at the airport, still wondering about this sudden change of circumstances.

After settling back in London for Term 2, Rose wrote a long letter to Nabeel telling him of her decision. She stressed that marriage and leaving her job was life-changing for her. She would not resign if he had any doubts about this being a lifelong relationship. She did not want any repeats of the story she had heard about Joseph's wedding. Nabeel was over the moon and told her he would go to the British Council, where he had some contacts to find a job for her. This was reassuring. She would be able to continue with her career and have some financial independence until they had children, which she assumed would be quite soon after their marriage, given their ages. She was in her late twenties, while Nabeel was already in his mid-thirties. Rose's body clock was ticking and pushing her previous ideas aside.

Within a short time she received an application form from the British Council for her to submit to the Central HQ in Spring Gardens, London. There was an accompanying letter from an official at the British Council, Kuwait. He explained that they would be opening a new school in November of the same year and so they were looking to appoint staff who would be able to set up the school in September. It seemed a heaven-sent opportunity for Rose, and helped to confirm her decision though she had to admit she was still suffering from doubts about the strength of her commitment to Nabeel.

Meanwhile work was as demanding as ever, with the long days and the added burden of her part-time TESOL course. She attended course meetings once a week, on Wednesday mornings, but she had to undergo a practical examination as well as submit a lengthy dissertation to obtain the qualification. It was now more important than ever to achieve this, so as to boost her CV for the British Council application.

Easter came and went with little diversion for Rose, but she had to set in motion the wedding plans. Nabeel had told her he was very busy and extremely successful in his individual efforts in the brothers' joint business enterprise in Kuwait. He would not be able to return to the UK until the wedding, which she should arrange for the end of August. To her relief he told her he was happy with a civil ceremony. She found out from the nearest Registry Office that she could book a date and time for the wedding, and did so. They could pay the fees on the day. She planned to give a self-catering lunch for family and an evening party for friends. They would obviously have to organise packing and shipping of their possessions to Kuwait, so life would be hectic in August. She couldn't find the courage to submit her resignation early. She decided to wait until her qualification was complete before she did so. When the desired result was awarded Rose breathed a sigh of relief and trepidation. The end of teaching was approaching and Rose knew she had to present her resignation letter to her boss soon. When she did so, he was upset and told her exactly what he was thinking:

"Don't you know you could be a Principal of an AEI in a couple of years? By the time you're 30 you'd command a terrific salary. How can you give up your career here now?"

Rose was equally upset at his reaction, because it raised the issue of her decision again. Had she done the right thing, she asked herself? She really was taking a step into the dark. She had never been to Kuwait and she had no idea what it would be like to live there. Her only saving grace was the new job. She had been called for interview to Spring

Gardens and she hoped what she learned there would bode well for the future.

The British Council HQ in central London was an impressive building. Rose made herself known to the receptionist and was directed to the interview room. There were no other candidates, which was hardly surprising given the location. Kuwait is a Muslim state which follows Saudi Arabia in strictly enforcing the prohibition of alcohol. The country's laws were not strictly Sharia but did include the death penalty for murder and flogging and deportation for the possession and/or transportation of alcohol. Rose was not yet fully aware of how these laws would impact on her life, but given her liking for wine and whisky she knew they would. For the time being, however, she was focussed on the job and its requirements. The job title was Senior Teacher. It did not sound very impressive, so she needed to know if the position would be an asset in her career development and increase her experience of ESOL.

The interviewer was a short, stocky man with a dark beard and a warm smile. Philip was to be her colleague, in the role of English Language Officer for the country, if she was chosen to undertake the position. He and a female staff member had copies of Rose's CV and their questions focussed mainly on the kind of work she was doing with the students. However, Philip seemed impressed by her venture into teacher training, both for ESOL teachers, and also with literacy volunteers. When it came time for Rose to ask the questions, she found out that prior to the setting up of this new centre the school had been operated from a small villa, only teaching Embassy officials on their own premises. There had not been public classes in the British Council's recent history. The new school was an ambitious venture and Philip was looking for someone with both practical experience and theoretical knowledge to take up the post of Senior Teacher. He intimated that she had sufficient skills in both areas for him to be able to offer her the post. Full details of the offer were to be communicated by mail.

By the end of the interview both parties felt they had learned a lot about each other. Rose had explained that she was leaving her career post only because she was getting married. She did not realise at the time that she was stepping into an economic trap, known as the local contract. In her *naivete* she had assumed that the details of the work were all she needed to know. Much later, at post in Kuwait she realised she was one of the cheap-rate personnel employed on local, rather than overseas contracts, losing the right to air tickets and accommodation allowances. Leaving the Inner London Education Authority for the British Council she felt she would be joining another organisation which had influence and career positions around the world, which eased her mind to a large extent about the major life and career change she was about to make. She hoped that knowing her future colleague even in a small way would help ease her into the job in Kuwait.

The interview and the follow up letter offering her the position served as a Crossing the Rubicon moment. She was not just leaving her job to get married: She was undertaking a new stage in her career with the world-famous British Council. They and International House were the major employers as well as change agents in worldwide ESOL, and she felt proud to be joining them. It made up for the loss she was experiencing in London. Her boss still was displeased but he had to accept that she was moving on. Rose was not asked to participate in her replacement's recruitment process, but she did organise an end of year leaving party for students and part-time staff, which the Principal attended, accepting, if unwillingly, her decision to leave.

20

Wedding Preparations

THE MORNING AFTER the school party Rose realised she needed to face up to reality. She was definitely going to Kuwait and she ought to pull herself together and stop questioning her decision. It was too late now to reverse her decision without looking stupid. She was going to have to put up with it. She had a job to go to in Kuwait and she needed to prepare herself for that and her new life. She began going through the possessions accumulated in her flat so as to be ready for the packers who would come in after the wedding was over. The garden flat which they had worked so hard on was now promised to friends of her brother. They had been given an inventory of the things Nabeel and Rose were leaving behind, and they had agreed to purchase them. The only item not on the inventory was Rose's piano. She hoped that one day she would be able to have it back, but who knew where or when?

During her perusal of the shelves she found a box of photos Nabeel had kept of his old flames, including Heidi. In a fit of jealous rage Rose shredded the photos and put them in the bin. If Nabeel noticed they were missing, she would challenge him about keeping them. Neither of them had many clothes or books in the flat at this point, but Rose had all her study papers from the three diploma courses she had taken in London. She decided to try to keep as much as possible in case the material came in handy in Kuwait. Nabeel had negotiated a good rate with an international moving company to pack and ship their possessions and a few items of furniture.

Back home in Rose's bedroom in the Midlands there were boxes of books and papers from Rose's degree in French. She decided not to take these as Mum had plenty of room for them. Also, there were boxes of treasures from Rose's youth, including her yellow Brownie tie, her blue Girl Guide tie and the badges she had attained while she was living with Dad and Mum in Berry Vale, and school photos, hockey and tennis team photos from her grammar school. Rose preferred to leave these *in situ* as she had no idea what kind of home they would have once they had settled in Kuwait. After all, she was planning to return home regularly, so she could take back anything she needed later. She left other treasured possessions behind, such as her little dancer Swiss Chalet musical box and other special presents from Mum.

In his letters Nabeel was full of good news about his business. He had focussed his energy on becoming a commission agent and local representative for several UK, USA and European companies which sold their products to the pipeline industry. Flares, pollution prevention, pig cleaners for pipelines, had been added to his knowledge base and forged-steel pipes, valves and flanges were now an established part of his repertoire when he visited the purchasing officers of KOC in the oil village of Ahmadi and KNPC in the city. Edouard, his older brother was also involved in sales but they kept their products separate so that they could manage their own finances independently under the same umbrella. Rose was pleased that he was doing well. It reinforced the idea that the world was their oyster and with her own job they would have a happy and successful family life. There had been one strange incident, however, when one of her Turkish friends passed on a phone message from Nabeel's former girlfriend, Heidi in Germany. Rose wondered again if something was going on, but then remembered her own secret assignation. They both had secrets, but the past was behind them. The future mattered more. She would not raise the issue.

Other practical considerations after booking the registry office for the wedding ceremony included what she would wear. This wedding had to be self-financing, so Rose decided to make her own dress. She wondered whether she should wear white, given her status now as a non-virgin, something she took more seriously than most at the time. After looking at materials and dress patterns in John Lewis' of Oxford Street she decided on oyster-coloured silk for a frilled neck,sleeveless dress which could be worn off the shoulder for the evening party, and white satin for a scoop-necked, short-sleeved dress for the ceremony and lunch. Even with her minimal finances a change of dress was appropriate for an all day celebration.

Mum and John were to come and stay in the flat for a few days before the ceremony and were to leave the day after. Dad, his wife and teenage daughter came to stay for a short visit a couple of weeks earlier, so that they could say their farewells. Rose's little sister seemed happy to have a vinyl record of the Beach Boys as a gift, as well as to visit some of the sights in London with her parents.

As well as packing, sewing, menu planning, and purchasing and preparing food Rose had to consider the guest list. The evening party was open to all. There would be plenty of space provided the weather was good. Selecting guests for the lunch party was more challenging. Rose's elderly French student friends lived in North London, and would prefer to travel during the day time so they were invited for lunch. Aunty Marie generously made a three tier traditional wedding cake with a small silver vase of fresh flowers on the top. Rose did not have the funds to buy wedding rings. She joked that they would use curtain rings if Nabeel did not arrive in time to purchase them.

In fact he arrived just two days before the big day and went straight out the next day to buy matching gold rings. The night before the wedding day they all went to bed, tired out. The next morning, the phone rang early. Unsuspecting, Rose answered, to hear Edouard's polite but formal voice: "Is Nabeel there, please?"

"Yes of course," Rose said, shaking Nabeel's shoulder, "here he is."

The ensuing conversation was in Arabic. Rose watched Nabeel's face lose colour as he listened, then spoke. When he had put the phone down, she asked "What's up?"

"Adel has crashed and rolled his car. They want me to go back."

"Really? Don't they know you are getting married?" she asked incredulously. After all her doubts then all her planning, she now thought this wedding might not take place. It was incredible, but her doubts appeared to have been well founded. Was this party going to be a wedding celebration or simply a party celebrating her narrow escape from marriage? She stared at Nabeel, words failing her.

"Is Adel injured? Is he in hospital?" she stammered.

"Well, he was checked out but he's back home now. He's OK, just shocked."

"So why do they need you? Is it a pretext for getting you back to Kuwait?"

"I don't think so. They just wanted to let me know what happened."

"OK, so what are you going to do?" she asked, quietly.

"I'm going to get married, of course," he laughed. "Don't be silly. Why waste these lovely rings?"

Rose began to relax. Perhaps she was making too much of it. This was her wedding day, a day she had never imagined would take place, but which was about to happen. It was like a dream, or a nightmare, she was not sure which. Since the decision, Mum, with her unusual sense of humour, had enjoyed singing a '50s comedy song, "I went to your wedding...we laughed...at last we got rid of you" which had increased rather than reduced Rose's stress levels. Mum, of course, was only joking, a phrase Nabeel used often.

"OK, on with the show. We have guests to look after. Bill's coming round at 10 to drive us to Fulham. As Edith Piaf sings, *"Je ne regrette rien."* At least not now, hey? Maybe later."

With that, the day's timetable kicked in, the plans went into action, and by the end of the day, many bottles of wine had been drunk, a lot of food enjoyed, the sun had shone brilliantly, the delicious cake had been cut and the deed was done with no regrets. The top tier of the cake was carefully wrapped, to be used as was British tradition, for the baptism of their first born. Rose breathed a big sigh of relief. Now she could get on with the cleaning, tidying, packing and prepare for the honeymoon in Egypt and their new home in Kuwait. She had never been to either country, but she knew she would be seeing the Pyramids and the Sphynx, which excited her immensely. She looked forward to being in Cairo for a week before flying to Kuwait, in the Persian, aka Arabian, Gulf.

Kuwait was more of a puzzle. Oil had been discovered in the desert in 1938 and the pearl fishing village had been transformed very rapidly by the newfound wealth into a modern city state. There were now excellent educational, medical and social systems for residents, but alcohol was prohibited by the state religion, Islam. There was no liquor allowance for Christians, whether visitors or residents. Rose enjoyed wine and whisky and wondered how she would cope without being able to purchase these legally. Nabeel had told her there was a black market, but access to it was not easy and prices were exorbitant.

They were setting up home with almost no funds. For their income they were relying on a deal which Nabeel had made, and the financial settlement was in the offing. Of course, Rose had already secured a job and Nabeel lived with his family, so the financial aspect did not concern her. She expected that side of life to be taken care of by her husband. She had made the decision to marry, to enter the cage she had dreaded, and now anticipated some of the joys of a permanent partnership: love, affection, support and in the future, a couple of children. But for now, she continued to keep the little pink pills by her bedside.

Epilogue

There was a mystery surrounding that wedding day phone call from Kuwait. Years later Nabeel insisted that he had told his family he was getting married. His family insisted that he had not. Whether Adel's car crash was simply an excuse to cancel the wedding and get Nabeel back to Kuwait again or whether there was really grave concern about Adel's state of health, Rose never discovered. The Lebanese Civil War had begun a year earlier and perhaps the family were concerned that bringing a British woman into the family would create their own familial conflict.

In retrospect, Rose could see their six-year London relationship was one of co-dependency. Neither was sure of their identity. They both needed the other to give them confidence and a sense of security as they progressed in the early, stressful stages of their careers. They had the same sense of agency in their work. They had bonded over time despite their ups and downs and on Rose's side, despite her long-held resistance to marriage she chose to marry with her head more than her heart. Her biological urge to have children pushed her to make a choice to stay with the partner she knew, rather than risk never meeting another compatible with her strengths and weaknesses.

Life is a journey, on which a series of choices presents itself. One must choose wisely. Rose's advice to others faced with a challenging decision is: **When in doubt, leave it out.** Don't be pressured by anyone to make an important decision. Take your time. Ask those close to you for their input but don't take it at face value. But above all, listen to your heart as well as your head. Human beings are emotional as well as intellectual. To paraphrase the sociologist Giddens, we construct our own cages and we can deconstruct them if necessary. Similarly, we can change ourselves, be change agents rather than victims of change. Our selves can be flexible according to our environment, but our core values persist.

Rose began this long 'writing cure' for two reasons: First, to identify the causes of her annual depression. The commemoration of Anzac Day is still enough to reduce her to tears, but Mum's death is now a familiar sadness and she has got used to the sound of duckshooting. Moreover, her 'baby' brother has returned to the family, so the sadness is now mitigated by joy.

The second reason was to control her temper. She found a book online: *As A Man Thinketh*, penned in the nineteenth century by James Allen, a British Midlander, like herself.

Vic Johnson uses the book on his personal development website, *AsAManThinketh.net*. Rose found this quote from Allen's book helpful:

"...humanity surges with uncontrolled passion, is tumultuous with ungoverned grief, is blown about by anxiety and doubt. ...Keep your hands firmly upon the helm of thought.... Self-control is strength. ... Calmness is power. Say unto your heart, 'Peace, Be still.'"*

*Day by Day with James Allen, by Vic Johnson, 2009, published by SYLVIA'S FOUNDATION INC., Florida, USA.